UNDER THE NOCTURNE MOON

2 NOCTURNE FALLS UNIVERSE STORIES

LARISSA EMERALD

UNDER THE NOCTURNE MOON
Compilation copyright © 2017 Larissa Emerald
The Vampire Bounty Hunter's Unexpected Catch © 2017 Larissa Emerald
The Shaman Charms the Shifter © 2017 Larissa Emerald

Published in the United States of America.

OTHER BOOKS BY LARISSA EMERALD

PARANORMAL ROMANCE

Nocturne Falls Universe
The Witch's Snow Globe Wish
in Merry & Bright: A Christmas Anthology

Divine Tree Guardian Series
Awakening Fire
Awakening Touch
Awakening Storm

Vampire – Blood Keepers Series
Forever At Dawn (novella)
Forever At Midnight (novella)

ROMANTIC SUSPENSE

Chalet Romance Series
Winter Heat

CONTEMPORARY ROMANCE

Barefoot Bay Kindle World
Come Sail Away

Want to stay up-to-date on upcoming books, release dates, giveaways, and contests from Larissa Emerald?

Sign up for her NEWSLETTER!
http://www.larissaemerald.com/newsletter

For Kristen,
for creating the awesomely funny Nocturne Falls stories.

Dear Reader,

Nocturne Falls has become a magical place for so many people, myself included. Over and over I've heard from you that it's a town you'd love to visit and even live in! I can tell you that writing the books is just as much fun for me.

With your enthusiasm for the series in mind—and your many requests for more books—the Nocturne Falls Universe was born. It's a project near and dear to my heart, and one I am very excited about.

I hope these new, guest-authored books will entertain and delight you. And best of all, I hope they allow you to discover some great new authors! (And if you like this book, be sure to check out the rest of the Nocturne Falls Universe offerings.)

In the meantime, happy reading!

Kristen Painter

For more information about the
Nocturne Falls Universe, visit
http://kristenpainter.com/sugar-skull-books.

CONTENTS

The Vampire Bounty Hunter's Unexpected Catch

A Nocturne Falls Universe Story

Can a vampire dance and shoot at the same time?

Vampire bounty hunter Nathaniel Newburg follows his mark into Nocturne Falls, a place where it's easy for anyone to hide and blend in. At first it seems as though he has his prey cornered, only to confront a beautiful feline-shifter Camille Nahuel instead. She dances around the floor with sultry steps, instructing a ballroom class, and dances around his heart even faster. Oh, Tango, the game is on. Can Nathaniel control his annoyance long enough to finish his job and save his love?

1

1

The grinding wheel shot out fiery sparks as Nathaniel worked. The knife was shaping up nicely and in its final stage before polishing and mounting the handle. He leaned in, examining the blade for imperfections. There were none. *Good.*

He carefully rested the knife on a stand and relaxed back in his barstool. His basement workshop was dry and well lit. That was not the case outside, though, where the wind rapped against the upstairs windows. His supernatural vampire-hearing made him aware of everything in the vicinity, including the howling weather.

The frigid storm whipped through Terror, Minnesota, dumping freezing rain and ice on the blackhearted town. He didn't mind the cold; however, he detested the rain.

Tomorrow morning, the ice-coated trees and landscape would sparkle as rays of sunlight struck the frozen shards, making everything glisten. Just like a fairy tale...

What a crock.

He sighed, forcing his thoughts back to the knife. The harsh winters in Minnesota were boring. There was only so much reading and TV he could endure; knife-making filled the void. It had proved to be a fine hobby throughout the centuries. Besides, superior weapons were necessary in his line of work. And he'd vowed over a century ago that he would never again be without the best.

He hung his head for a second as he allowed his failure to protect his brother, Jake, to wash over him with the same raw ache it always did, even after 140 years. Which was as it should be. He was not the one in a wheelchair.

The memory of the vampire war all those years ago leaped to the surface of his mind. The incident had happened at the onset of the war, and had occurred without warning. A loco vamp had attacked Jake, stabbing him with a wooden stake. Only he hadn't been struck in his heart, but rather an inch lower, sending the stake straight through his spinal cord. The only weapon Nathaniel had brought with him was his bare hands. And while he'd broken the rogue's neck, it had been too little too late for his brother.

There were things worse than death, and being a vampire in a wheelchair was one of them.

He picked up the knife again. As he pressed its metal edge against the grinder once more, his cell phone whistled, letting him know he had a message. He glanced over at it and read the text:

Meet me at Fortune's in thirty minutes.

What? Damn...

The text was from a longtime friend in San Francisco, vampire leader Connor Langley. But what was the czar doing in Terror?

Nathaniel reluctantly stood. He didn't relish traipsing out in this weather, but he was a Minnesotan and used to it. Besides, one didn't reject a request from a powerful vampire commander. He sighed and put away his tools.

Regardless of his mild irritation at having to go out, a half hour later, the rain had changed to a light snowfall as Nathaniel strolled down Omen Avenue, the main street in Terror. His footfalls echoed off the brick sidewalk and were swallowed by the hazy fog that touched everything. Streetlamps glowed like beacons lighting the way, even as the gothic buildings loomed over the few pedestrians traveling the street with him. In the middle of the block, he ducked into Fortune's Pub, which was adjacent to the only major upscale hotel in town, the Misery Inn.

Inside, Barbarella, a Neko Demi-Cat who had worked at the place since graduating high school, greeted him and escorted him to a booth near the raging fire. Connor and a female who Nathaniel didn't recognize were already seated.

"Scotch," he said over his shoulder to Barbarella.

"Coming right up."

Then he took in Langley. "I'm shocked you're here. If I recall, you don't like the cold weather."

Connor snickered, his blue eyes intense. "*Hate* is more accurate." He stood, clasped Nathaniel's hand, and initiated a shoulder bump. "However, we're crossing the country on our return from abroad, and I'm calling in every favor owed to me."

They each took a seat in the booth. The waitress slid his drink onto the table and left.

"Nate, this is my wife, Stephanie," Connor said as he slid one arm around the lovely blonde at his side. She smiled and leaned into his massive frame.

"Pleased to meet you. Congratulations." Nathaniel raised his glass in a salute, and they all drank. He hadn't kept track of the vampire leader, so his marriage news was certainly a revelation. Especially since he had married a human female. Nathaniel inhaled deeply, catching a whiff of the woman's sweet scent.

"Thank you," Stephanie said. "I've heard a lot about you."

"Don't believe everything you hear." Nathaniel downed the remainder of his Scotch and caught the waitress's attention with a wave of his hand, signaling for another round. "Perhaps I should tell you a few things about your husband." He shot Connor a pointed look, thinking back to the vampire rebellion of 1810.

Connor cleared his throat and got right to the point. "I have a job for you, Bounty Hunter."

"Yeah? What's that?"

"We've been having a problem with someone selling cobine on the black market. They've been stockpiling it and driving the price incredibly high, making it difficult to get. I got word that someone—a rogue vampire by the name of Payton Grey—may have some connections to it, or even be running it himself. My latest intel says he's in your area. I need you to bring him to me. *Alive.*"

Nathaniel paused beneath the arched entrance to his house, buttoning his double-breasted gr*eat coat and sliding on his leather gloves. For days, he'd been canvassing Terror, questioning people about the whereabouts of Payton Grey. Some males knew of Grey, but so far every lead had turned into a wild-goose chase.

He tromped across the front lawn. His heel

slipped, but he kept walking. The ice-crusted snow snapped and cracked in the woods next door.

Damned rain.

From what he'd learned, Payton came from a young group of veaklings out in Nevada. The vampire race had been diluted over the years, and veaklings were at the bottom of the gene pool. At the top were the original ancestors, who had traveled from the planet Cest and had extremely pure bloodlines, like Connor, and then there were semi-purists, the category that Nathaniel belonged to. Their blood was pure enough to respect the old ways, and they had enough control not to feed on humans.

The different factions of vampires and their ancestries determined how they related in society, how they tolerated sunlight, how they controlled their bloodlust. And the veaklings... They lacked control, values, *and* purpose.

Nathaniel had put out the call to the Vulcan Society, an elite underground group of paranormal beings who had banded together centuries before to protect the secrecy of supernaturals. Someone had to have seen the vampire. His friends had been doing a foot search, when a text had finally come. Payton was stocking up at the Hell's Fire Liquor Store.

Nathaniel pulled his coat tighter about himself and quickly traced to Hell's Fire. He hurried inside and looked around the store, but even though mere minutes had passed, it seemed Payton had already fled. Still, his scent was fresh enough for Nathaniel to latch on to it.

He took a deep inhale and followed the smell. Eventually, it stopped when he reached a barn on the outskirts of Terror. He scanned the area, noticing an open door. He crept over to it and looked inside. A human body, positioned over a bale of hay, had been drained at the neck and smelled of whisky.

Damn.

Nathaniel ground his teeth and punched the wall next to him. His hand went clear through the old wood, leaving a splintered hole when he withdrew it. That stupid vamp was totally out of control.

Nathaniel sighed, trying to pick up the liquor-spiced scent of the vampire once more. It was faint, but it was there, and he followed it again, this time across the field beside the shack and deep into the woods.

Camille Nahuel eased back the studio curtain and peeked outside. People were beginning to walk the streets, as they would on any regular Halloween night, except it wasn't actually Halloween. But that was the charm of Nocturne Falls, Georgia: every day was Halloween. And after living there for over a year, she'd finally gotten used to it.

The place was busier than usual for midweek, but then with the Mardi Gras Ball on Friday, out-of-towners were coming in early. Her Wednesday-evening ballroom class would begin arriving in a few minutes. She twisted the door lock, and the bolt disengaged with a click. As she pulled her hand back, her thumbnail snagged on the edge of the lock and ripped.

Ow!

She jerked her hand away and shook it at the throbbing pain. Squinting, she examined the nail, torn down to the quick. A thread of blood showed along the break line and oozed across her green-glitter nail polish.

Not the best way to start the evening. Many supernaturals were sensitive to the odor of blood, with vampires and werewolves among the most volatile.

Her feline nature surfacing, Camille ran her tongue over the wound and drew it into her mouth for a second, then removed it, checking the wound again. She grimaced. At the slightest bump tonight, that would be it—the nail would be toast.

As a precaution, she retrieved a Band-Aid from a box near the CD player. She chuckled at the ironic jaguar print she'd found on the Internet. This was her first opportunity to use them. When she finished wrapping the wound, she extended her hand, admiring the bandage.

Yep. So stinkin' cute.

She glanced up and down her arm, watching as the jag spots that had dimly risen to the surface faded. Hmm. She still needed more control over that glimmer. But lately it seemed as though she'd reverted to her wild college days at Clemson, where she'd earned degrees in business and history. Her emotions were running just under the surface, and she was feeling that searching urge again, that drive to find something more to life than simple existence.

The front door opened then, and Julian Ellingham strolled in. A vampire with a slim face, high cheekbones, and hair the color of midnight, he had powerful shoulders and a greater-than-god attitude. He was all charm and personality. The town's biggest playboy, too, rumor had it. But he'd directed a ton of customers to her doorstep so she tried to be grateful, despite her feelings toward him. Or toward all vamps, actually.

Almost on his heels, a small group of six regulars entered. Camille rented the small room from Mrs. Turner, and it really wouldn't accommodate many more students than that. During the morning hours, other instructors occupied the space, offering classes like yoga and karate.

Alex Cruz flashed Camille a handsome grin as

he walked in. A panther shifter and one of the town's deputies, he was one of her favorite students. He had a quiet demeanor for someone in law enforcement, she thought.

She looked around the room. Most of her students right now were there to brush up their dancing skills prior to the town's inaugural Mardi Gras Ball. But when her gaze landed on two female students, she couldn't help but wonder if they had signed up because of Alex. There were certainly a lot of doe-eyed glances coming from them. She did know that Alex had talked werewolf sheriff Hank Merrow and his wife, Ivy, into taking the class, though.

Camille sighed as she watched Julian shed his outer jacket and hang it up. To her dismay, vamps made the best students. They were quick learners, sophisticated, and as it turned out, they didn't mind parting with their money. She'd learned early on that the easiest way to make a profit was to cater to vamps, even if she didn't like it. Especially here in Nocturne Falls where the Ellingham family owned nearly half the town.

Hell's belles, her father must be rolling over in his grave.

But most paranormal beings here tried to get along at least. It was part of the reason she'd moved to Nocturne Falls. She'd discovered the code of ethics in town was pretty straightforward: don't mess up the town's facade of Halloween twenty-four seven, and mind your own business. And for the most part, it worked.

So she set aside her vampire hatred, telling herself the vamps here were different from the covens at home in New Orleans. She didn't really believe that—in her heart, every vampire turned into the one who had slayed her parents—but it helped her take their money with a smile.

One day she'd be able to vindicate her past...

She expelled another heavy sigh, telling herself she was more sensitive today than usual since it was the anniversary of their deaths. Eight years... Could it possibly have been that long?

She shook herself. Now was not the time to think about that. Instead, she plastered a smile on her face and began class. That was the thing about teaching: no matter how she felt, there was a certain amount of performance involved. If she had a headache, she still had to teach. If she had to put her dog down, she still had to go through the steps. And so she led the group through the warm-up exercises of the basics—box step, triple step, and rock step, along with walking with a partner. Then she segued into the individual dances. This evening's lesson was near the end of the semester, which meant less instruction and more dancing.

Couples who came to class together usually remained paired; however, solo students changed off. Camille took a turn with each male, though, and when they rotated partners for the fourth time, Alex stepped to the front. She enjoyed dancing with him more than the other males in class. His sleek panther reflexes easily transferred through his steps and were a good match to hers. He was a confident leader without being overbearing, as Julian tended to be.

"The next dance is a fox-trot," she announced, recalling the order of her music selections.

Alex took her hand, assuming the perfect frame, his free hand lightly touching her shoulder blade. He was a follow-the-rules guy, and he aimed to please.

She took a deep breath as they stepped off in unison and glided into a box step. He smelled of the woods, of pine and sage and earth—all scents she knew well. She kept expecting him to ask her out, but he never did. Why was that? Did he have a girlfriend she didn't know about? He'd never mentioned anyone…

His eyes met hers. "You're doing fantastic," she told him. She let her eyelids sweep down to his chest and then back to his face.

He gave her a boyish smile. "Thanks."

She glanced away, assessing her other students. "Nick, close your steps more and loosen up. Try not to be so stiff."

"Gotcha," he responded. But the gargoyle shifter's movements barely changed.

The song ended, and the partners separated. Camille used her Bluetooth remote to pause the music. "Go ahead and take a break. Get a drink before we do our last dance of the evening, which will be a waltz."

The students laughed and spoke softly to one another as they left the dance floor and gathered in small groups around the edges of the room. Camille grabbed a bottle of water off the table next to the sound system and took a sip. Julian followed her and did the same.

She noticed he drank a lot less water than the others did. Perhaps vampires didn't need to replace fluids in the same way.

"Cami, could we do something other than a waltz for our final dance?" he asked.

She tensed at his implied familiarity. "It's Camille. Only my dad called me Cami."

"Oh, I'm sorry."

She shrugged. He wouldn't have known it was a sore spot for her. She shook her head. "But to answer your question, no. I already have the music lined up. And it makes for a nice cool down to finish the evening."

His eyes flashed—in irritation, she thought—but he bent at the waist and bowed to her. "As you wish." He extended his hand, motioning for her to take the center of the floor.

"Take your places everyone," she said to the group.

She began the music and placed her hand in Julian's outstretched one. A shiver ran through her. And not the good kind…

He twirled her effortlessly around the dance floor, regardless, and she couldn't help but appreciate his grace. The next thing she knew, the waltz was finished and the students were packing up.

"Hey, everyone," she shouted over the din of their chatting. "Don't forget to sign up for next month. We'll be focusing on Latin dances."

Ivy nudged her husband. "Ooh, the tango. We need more of that!"

Hank rolled his eyes and then leaned in and whispered something in her ear that made her blush crimson as they headed for the door.

A typical couple thing.

The rest of her students left in small waves, though Julian lagged behind.

"I need to ask you something," he said.

Camille hesitated, her back to him as she shut down the sound system. Was he going to ask her to the ball? The absurd idea flitted through her thoughts. She sure hoped not.

When she couldn't put it off any longer, she turned to face him. Over his shoulder, she saw Alex pause at the door. Now *that's* who she wanted to go out with.

She waved to him and smiled. "Bye, Alex."

He nodded at her, then exited. When she glanced back at Julian, the vampire's jaw was pulsing. Had he picked up on her interest? Living among paranormal beings was much tougher than living among humans. Their senses were sharper, keener. And they perceived things a girl sometimes wanted to hide.

"What's up?" she asked.

His head angled abruptly to the side, as if he'd heard something that piqued his interest or distracted him. He stepped back and toward the window. "Never mind. I'll catch you later."

He spun on his heel and tromped out the door. His odd behavior left her wondering if he'd picked up on a scent or perhaps some trouble in the streets. Since he was usually Vampire On Duty for the nighttime entertainment crowd, she figured his reaction must have something to do with his work.

A tingle of apprehension lifted the hairs on her nape. She inhaled a long, slow, calming breath and swept her gaze across the empty studio. She was being ridiculous. No one was there.

She grabbed her things and tugged open the front door, ready to go home. As she reached for the light switch something brushed her arm, and she gasped, a scream caught in her throat.

2

Every creature had its own scent, whether human, or werewolf, or Valkyrie, or vampire. It was the difference between an elephant and a giraffe, and they almost always left a trail of some sort behind them as they moved. One just needed to know the signs. And any good bounty hunter knew how to track them.

Payton Grey traced not far ahead. Older and more experienced vampires could trace a greater distance—a hundred miles at a time, perhaps—but Grey could only average around fifty or so. Which meant he was either young, injured, needing to feed, or suffering from a lack of cobine. And since he reportedly had commandeered the latter, Nathaniel didn't think that was it.

Nathaniel had traced Grey across the country as the crow flies since he'd left the shack outside of Terror, following him from pit stop to pit stop and closing the guy's three-hour lead. Coming to rest on the edge of a cornfield in southwestern Indiana, his gaze followed the coppery scent of blood floating on the night breeze.

The white of an animal's tail caught his attention first. The dead rabbit was tucked between two dried and spent cornstalks. Nathaniel turned it over with the toe of his boot, and its neck flopped to the side, ragged and bloody. The bite had ripped a large gash in its throat.

The act spoke of unpreparedness and perhaps desperation. He shook his head. He wouldn't waste any more time. Grey's scent continued south, and so would he. He willed himself into the trace, again following the particles in the air that held the essence of the young veakling.

By the time he reached Tennessee, he surmised his prey was heading for either Nocturne Falls or New Orleans. Both were killer places to hide, but he was hoping for the latter. Last he'd heard, Jake had a place in Nocturne Falls, and he wasn't planning on visiting his brother.

The pungent scent veered eastward for several miles, then turned south again.

If his instincts were correct, the gap between him and Grey drilled down to less than fifteen minutes. He didn't linger at this touch point but pressed onward.

As he passed over the mountain ranges with updrafts and smoky mist, he had to concentrate even harder to stay on the trail. The veakling made another easterly turn, which could only mean one thing: his destination was Nocturne Falls. Nathaniel had never been there, but all paranormal creatures knew of the town that celebrated Halloween all year round.

And sure enough, when he reached the city limits, the sign read, WELCOME TO NOCTURNE FALLS—WHERE EVERY DAY IS HALLOWEEN.

Entering the town, he slowed his pace. Not because he wanted to but because of the intrusion of many other scents. He was so close. The rogue vampire was near. He could feel it. And yet it instantly became difficult to distinguish Grey's particular essence.

Nathaniel jogged down Shadows Drive, turning his head to the right, then left. His senses were overwhelmed by supernatural beings of every kind—shifters, witches, vampires, and more. You name the creature, and it was probably there.

He stopped when he came to the fountain in the middle of town. The smell of the water floated on the air, cleansing it. He closed his eyes, shutting out all the people and creatures walking along the streets and shops. He allowed his instincts to rule, moving forward and turning down Jack O'Lantern Lane.

There. Grey's stench…blanketed with that of the dead rabbit's.

Nathaniel's pulse ramped up in his anticipation of the forthcoming confrontation. He moved quickly along the walk when suddenly the scent was gone. He halted, then swept his gaze in an arc. Nothing. The veakling must have turned already.

Nathaniel backtracked until he scented Grey once more. Nathaniel turned into a shop—Camille's Ballroom Dancing, he noted from a portable sign.

Was Grey hiding inside?

The door opened as the lights went out, and Nathaniel grabbed the wrist extending past the doorframe.

The sound of a gasp and the floral scent tickling his nose didn't match up with his mark. He scrunched his brow. He'd been tracing for an awfully long time, after all. He hadn't realized his level of fatigue. Then it registered that the wrist he was holding was of the female variety.

Definitely *not* his prey.

"Let go of me," Camille screeched.

"The vampire. Where did he go?"

She tugged at her wrist, trying to get free. "I'll call the sheriff."

"Did he come inside? His scent is close."

Camille couldn't help herself, and she inhaled, simply to verify what he had said. Sure enough, there was a strange odor on the air. But that didn't mean she knew anything about it.

"No one came inside. And I'm leaving for the evening. Please get out of my way."

Instead, he held on tight. His fingers thrummed against her pulse point, as if he were tuning a guitar. Whatever was going through his mind, she didn't know, but when he finally released her, he didn't step away. His large, muscular frame remained, blocking her exit.

"I'm sorry," the stranger said. "I didn't mean to startle you. I'm after someone, and he came in this direction."

She tilted her head up, searching his eyes through the darkness. A car circled the fountain down the lane, illuminating him with its headlights. She had feline night vision and, like most paranormal beings, could see extremely well even in pitch-black conditions. As the lights passed over him, his eyes shone an amber-gold and his fangs elongated with a wicked hint of a smile. Was this his attempt at beguiling her?

No, she didn't have time to go down that thoughtful road.

He reached above her head and forced the door open, pushing her back inside the room. "Do you mind if I have a quick look around?"

She swallowed hard. Yes! She minded a lot!

But it must not have really been a question, because he didn't wait for her answer. He advanced, and she sidestepped to get out of his way, her irritation growing greater than her fear.

His footsteps echoed as he moved farther into the empty space. She didn't take her eyes off him while she flipped on the light switch with trembling fingers.

"I already told you: no one is here," she bit out, her voice anything but timid now.

And then she got her first good look at him. Air rushed into her lungs, and her breath caught. He was definitely handsome, but it was the scoped rifle slung across his shoulder that shocked her the most. Of their own volition, her claws extended and her jaguar spots glimmered.

He held up a hand to shield his eyes from the sudden bright light. "Ugh. You didn't have to go and do that."

She narrowed her gaze on him. "Take your look around and get out."

He stared at her, his vision seeming to quickly adjust. She placed one balled fist on her hip and shifted her weight. As she stared back at him, she straightened and crossed her arms. He was a vampire—no surprise there—tall and powerfully built with blond, chin-length hair.

Run-your-fingers-through-it hair...

She lowered her hands and clasped them in front of her.

His brows were darker than his hair, his eyes hooded, his nose straight, and his lips on the full side. He had two days' worth of stubble on his face. A black leather jacket, unbuttoned and open, showed off his physique, and a suede messenger bag was slung across his chest.

He spun around and checked the closet, bathroom, and corners. "Did you know a vampire can hang out in mid-trace? Essentially suspended?"

God, he carries all that muscle and authority well.

She tried to keep her voice even. "Yes. I know. Now can we be going?"

He sighed and led the way out. She flipped off the light and locked the door, even though it made her uneasy to have her back to him. She could feel his watchful eyes taking in her every move.

"You might want to check down the alley," she said when she turned around.

He glared in that direction, his brow pinched, pensive and unsympathetic. "No. He's gone."

She started to leave, moving around him toward the fountain and the people walking the streets.

"Wait," he said.

She didn't want to, but her feet obeyed. She

didn't look over her shoulder, though. Just looked straight ahead. His clothes rustled, and she heard his steps as he came up behind her to stand at her left. She flicked a glance in his direction as he reached into his bag and produced a business card. He handed it to her.

"The rogue vampire I'm looking for could be dangerous. If you see anyone new or suspicious lurking around town, call me."

A chuckle escaped her lips. "You haven't been in Nocturne Falls long, have you?" Since she didn't really care what his answer was, she rushed on. "There are strangers trolling the streets every night here."

"If you see him, you'll know it. He has a tattoo of a snake on his neck."

Camille shivered. She hated snakes even more than she hated vampires.

Nathaniel laughed under his breath as she hustled down the street. Her light-brown hair swished across her back as she walked. His eyes slid lower, admiring the provocative sway of her hips. Feline shifters had a seductive stride like no other supernatural. He shook his head to clear it.

The silly, fearful girl… She had little to dread from him. He prided himself on being able to control himself, no matter the situation. It was a characteristic that made him a superior bounty hunter, and it was a quality he valued in others.

The vampire he chased didn't possess such an ability.

Slowly, he moved into the street and glanced in both directions. As long as he had been tracking Grey in the uncomplicated, earthy-scented outdoors, the vampire had been an easy target. But here it was much more difficult to distinguish his aroma. Sort of like separating out the smell of blueberry from a bowl of ambrosia.

He licked his lips, hungry. Since it seemed he would be staying at least the night, his next order of business was to find food and shelter.

Nathaniel strolled down Main Street, marveling at the town all decked out in mini-lights. He'd never seen so much orange and purple in his entire life. A few paranormal creatures played up to the crowd, assuming stereotypical roles. A werewolf harassed a grandma with gray hair, who gave a scream and then laughed. They were acting their parts for the humans, he realized. Live entertainment—it was the reason tourists flocked here.

Several people turned their heads as Nathaniel traveled along the center of the street as if he owned it. When he came to the Black Rose Dead and Breakfast, he marched up the wooden steps and headed inside. It was midweek, so hopefully it wasn't all booked up.

A small cubicle served as a front desk, and a short elfin woman looked him up and down with piercing brown eyes. "May I help you?" she asked.

"That depends. Do you have a vacant room?"

She smacked her wrinkled lips together. "That depends. Can you be courteous and well-mannered?" She slipped on wire-rimmed glasses, tucking them behind her pointed ears, and then peered at him over the lenses.

He flashed a smile and bowed slightly. "But of course."

"Hmph." She flipped a sheet of paper on the desk. "I have an upstairs room at the back. Has its own bath. One hundred a night."

Nathaniel raised an eyebrow.

"But I'll give you the vampire special of ninety dollars," she added.

"Thank you—" he read her name tag "—Mrs. Turnbuckle."

She gave a single sharp nod and pursed her lips as he handed over the bills for one night's stay. She counted it with flair, placed it in a drawer, and slid a key toward him. "Here you go."

He snatched it up. No electronic key cards here. As he tossed it in the air and caught it, he shot her a wink. "Thanks."

"Rascal," she muttered.

"The name's Nathaniel," he shot back over his shoulder.

She chuckled as he walked away.

Moving up the stairs and down the hallway, he paid attention to the sounds of the old house and its structural details, memorizing them. Which boards creaked beneath his weight? How far it was to his door? Was there a rear exit? Who else was staying here?

When he reached his room, he turned the key and slipped inside.

The place was decorated in classy gothic decor with cream-colored walls, wood floors, a deep burgundy-and-black bedspread, black curtains, and an electric, wrought iron candelabra on the nightstand. He got a chuckle out of the closet, which was a rough-hewn casket fixed to the wall. He removed his two changes of clothes from his messenger bag and gave them a shake before hanging them up.

Next, he unpacked his blood supply. The suite had a small refrigerator in the corner. A necessary perk since the place advertised that they catered to vamps. He stored the three vials he'd brought.

Mmm breakfast.

For the time being, he'd settle for the instant version. Not exactly to his liking, but it did the trick in a pinch. He got a glass of warm water from the sink, dumped in a packet of brownish-red powder, and stirred it with the back end of his toothbrush.

He wrinkled his nose at his first taste. The initial hit was always the worst. He only drank the stuff when he was on the road, and it took a swig or two to get used to the taste. As he swallowed, he thought of the human equivalent of chocolate milk or maybe one of those fruity, vitamin powder drinks. The latter he could at least tolerate.

His phone whistled. He swiped his thumb over the screen, revealing a message from Connor requesting an update. *Anxious bastard.*

Nathaniel scrolled on. He'd answer the missive when he'd caught the vampire, and only then.

Another swipe over the phone screen landed him on his brother's number. His finger hovered over the screen. He knew he really should call. Really should catch up. Really should put the past behind him.

But he stared at the screen until it went blank.

Nope.

He thrust it into his coat pocket.

With his lodging taken care of and something in his stomach, it was time to find Grey. In most cities, he would unearth the underground vampire faction, but here, things were right out in the open. Even still, he'd bet there were popular dives and hidden places where only the locals hung out. And he'd find them.

3

Camille needed a drink. Big-time. She eased into one of the Poisoned Apple's burgundy leather booths where her friend and fellow feline shifter, Caroline—CC for short—was waiting.

CC leaned on the table. "Freakin' Hour was almost up. I hope you don't mind, but I ordered you a Little Birdie."

"Two-for-one drinks," Camille said, without censoring her exasperation. "Perfect. Just what I need."

CC narrowed her eyes. "What happened?"

Camille brushed her hair behind an ear as she scanned the bar—just to be sure he wasn't there somehow. "This vamp from out of town rushed into the studio as I was locking up. Said he was after another vampire."

CC raised an eyebrow and smirked. "Anything kinky?"

Slipping out of her jacket, Camille shook her head. "No. He'll probably be on his way tomorrow." She inhaled deeply, allowing her chest to rise and fall. "But good heavens, for a bloodsucker, he sure was gorgeous. Fit, tall…and blond."

"Really? Oooh, one of those rare ones."

"I know, right?"

The waitress delivered their drinks, and CC paid her.

"The next one's on me," Camille said.

"'Kay." CC ran her tongue around the edge of her glass, licking the sugar. "So what else about this vamp?"

Camille sipped her drink. "What's in this anyway?" she asked, distracted by the coconut flavor swirling in her mouth.

Her friend shrugged. "Vodka, coconut rum, and lemon sorbet… I think." She paused, smacking her lips. "Back to my question."

Camille took another sip. "It was weird. The guy even gave me his card." She withdrew it from her purse and read it aloud. *"Nathaniel Newburg. Bounty Hunter."*

"Bounty Hunter?" CC scoffed. "Man, you can pick 'em."

"Hey, what does that mean? He ran into me, not the other way around," she defended. "I don't like vamps, and you know it." Her voice was now a whisper.

"Okay, okay…" CC said, raising a hand in submission. "So what do you want to do tonight?"

"Relax." She leaned back in her seat and let the coolness of the leather seep through her shirt.

"Let's barhop. Head over to Howler's and maybe shoot some pool or somethin'." Then she smiled. "I saw Kevin James going in when I passed."

"Checking out someone new?" Camille didn't want to dwell on CC's latest breakup—it would only bring her friend down—and luckily, it seemed CC didn't, either. "Sounds good to me."

The Poison Apple had a band playing that night, so Camille and CC both angled sideways in their seats and listened while they finished their drinks. After that, they headed a few streets over to Howler's and went to the back room where the pool tables and bar games were.

Sure enough, Kevin was there, leaning over a pool table, racking up a game. "Okay, who's next?" he asked the crowd.

The room grew silent as everyone looked around, taking in the other patrons. "I'm out," said Todd Grieves, a dragon shifter Camille had been interested in for a while. "I'm grabbing a burger."

Out of the corner of her eye, Camille saw CC step forward. But at the same time, someone else came out of the shadows—a vampire.

He was young and had a mean look about him. His cheeks dipped inward, lean and pronounced, and his jawline flared wide. He had a long face, but it wasn't narrow, and he had a mustache and goatee.

"I'll play you for some info on where to pick up a…meal," the stranger said.

Everyone in the room knew he was talking about where he could get blood. Camille was pretty sure there was only one place that served a vampire meal—Insomnia, a members-only club for supernaturals.

Kevin grinned. "That's easy. Let's get started."

CC's face fell as she lost her chance to go toe to toe with Kevin. But she recovered quickly and sauntered over for a good seat to watch the game.

Camille's gaze shot back to the vampire. He removed his jacket and stretched. As he turned to face her fully, her scrutiny landed on the snake tattoo slithering up his neck. He looked straight at her and tilted his head, almost as if he recognized her.

But she was the one who recognized him. *This* was the vampire the bounty hunter was looking for.

She swallowed and took a step backward. She watched as he hit the cue ball with such force, she thought it might disintegrate. And between every set, his black eyes returned to her.

Call the bounty hunter.

Camille edged closer to CC and whispered in her ear, "I'm going to the bathroom. Be right back."

The restroom was a long way from the pool area, back in the restaurant section of Howler's, but she briskly strolled to the other end and stopped near the kitchen. She hoped the noise there would be enough to drown out the conversation she was about to have. Her hand shook as she removed her phone and the business card from her pocket. So much so that it took her two tries to snag the slim edge of her cell and then hit the "call" button.

After glancing around, she considered the business card and entered the number, praying this was the smart thing to do.

"Nathaniel here," the vampire said in a reverberating tone.

Camille rushed into the conversation before she could change her mind. "This is Camille. We met today at my dance studio. I'm at Howler's, and the vampire you are searching for is here."

"Howler's?"

"Yes."

"Stay put," he ordered. Then the line went silent.

Camille had no sooner glanced up from her cell phone that she heard a loud *crack!* from the direction of the pool room. A second later, the snake-necked vampire paused in front of the restaurant entrance as he glared at her with glowing, defiant eyes. He snarled, displaying his fangs in silent promise. He'd heard her conversation.

She trembled, her heart beating in bursts.

Then he pushed his way outside and was gone.

When she could breathe again, she ran to the back room to see if CC and everyone else were okay. "What happened?" Camille asked.

CC placed her hand on Camille's. "He had some sort of temper tantrum, breaking the pool stick and throwing it across the room. That's all."

"I think he heard my call. He gave me the evil eye before he ran out the door. He was the one the bounty hunter was looking for. It was like he knew I was reporting him. I should have gone outside, maybe even down the road, to make that call," Camille whispered.

She shook her head. Kevin was setting up another game as if nothing had happened. She guessed many of the alpha males were used to such confrontations.

With a nudge of her chin toward Kevin, she said, "Go ahead and play. I'm going home."

CC didn't hesitate, saying, "Do you want me to go with you?"

"No. I'll be fine." She hugged CC good-bye. "I'll talk to you tomorrow."

When Camille stepped out of Howler's, there he was, an immovable wall, as if a boulder had dropped in front of her.

"He's gone," she said by way of explanation. "He must have heard me speaking to you because he fled as soon as I disconnected."

The bounty hunter left her and traced in a wide circle before returning, clearly trying to pick up his target's scent.

Standing next to her once more, he crossed his arms over his muscular chest. "Damn this town. There are so many different creatures that their odors interfere with one another."

She gave him a sympathetic look. "I'm sorry."

He shrugged. "It's okay. I'll catch him."

"And then what will you do with him?"

"Take him home to Minnesota."

"Oh my," she said, amazed. "You're a long way from home."

"Yes. But the weather is more agreeable here. I may stay awhile." He laughed, and she discovered it was a nice sound. Her insides did a series of flip-flops, and her unease lessened.

Still, he is a vampire and not to be trusted, her inner voice warned.

He smiled at her as if he knew the cause of her hesitation. But he could not know that a vampire had lured and betrayed her father, getting him killed. She stiffened at the memory.

"I'd like to repay you for calling me," he said, surprising her again. "Even though Grey got away, I appreciate your effort. May I buy you a drink?"

She shook her head. "I'm afraid I've had enough. And it's not necessary. Really."

"Something to eat, then? Have you eaten? You can help me get to know the town."

"I don't think so." She began to walk down the street.

"Dessert! How about ice cream?" His eyes grew darker.

She pursed her lips, wondering if he was doing the trance thing she'd heard vampires could do. Gosh, he sure was alluring. "You're not going to let this go, are you?"

He traced in front of her, making her stop, and gave her a smile. "No. I'm not."

It might have been the two Little Birdies she'd already had, but she glanced sideways, saying, "All right. The Ice Scream Shop is just around the corner."

4

The Ice Scream Shop garnered a quick turnover with most tourists making their selections and taking their desserts with them. And to Nathaniel's delight, the shop offered a bloody maraschino cherry sorbet. The bloody part consisted of an oozy cherry syrup drizzled on top. He was drooling just looking at it.

There were several wrought iron tables outside lining the street and adjacent alley. Once they'd ordered, Nathaniel chose one in the front corner, assuming Camille would rather be out in the open than tucked in the shadows, as he would have normally preferred. He pulled out a chair for her, and she set down the double-cream supreme chocolate sundae she'd selected before sitting down herself.

Nathaniel sat, as well, and took one bite of his ice cream. The full, tangy taste of cherries slid down his throat, and he instantly knew what they must serve in heaven. "Mmm, this is my new most favorite thing," he said. "I'm going make Nocturne Falls a regular pit stop when I travel."

"What's your old most favorite thing?" She peered at him from beneath her lashes and gave a soft laugh.

He smiled at her inquisitive question, somehow pleased that she was showing an interest in him. "Coffee. Dark, strong, and straight-up. With none of those frothy frills."

"Hmm. I like the frothy frills. Give me a caramel mocha any day," she said, her southern accent growing heavier.

He smiled. "I'm not shocked." He took another bite of his dessert. "Have you lived here long? Your accent reminds me of New Orleans."

"Pretty good guess, Bounty Hunter," she said with a smile. "I grew up there actually. Only moved here a year ago. After...after my parents died."

"I'm sorry to hear that." He leaned closer to her, wanting to slip his arm around her but restraining himself. He sensed she wouldn't allow it.

She lifted a shoulder and held it there for a moment before letting it fall back down. "Some things you just don't get over." Then her demeanor changed as she straightened in her chair. Her smile seemed to take effort, as if forced. "But I moved on. Now I have a new life in a new town."

He nodded. He definitely understood loss. And he understood it took time to heal.

He really should call Jake…

"Listen." He lowered his voice as he reached out and placed his hand over hers on the table, giving in to the strong desire to touch her. She didn't pull away, but she did tense. "I appreciate you helping me, but now I'm worried that Grey might retaliate. If he heard your phone call, then he's made the connection between you and me. And he's known to be brutal."

"I didn't consider that when I called. He just felt…wrong."

He gave a grateful smile, knowing exactly what she meant. "You have good instincts. Trust them." And on that note, he added, "Let me walk you home."

Her brows shot to her hairline in wonder.

"I only want to know that you're safe," he clarified.

She began to rise, and he got up quickly to help her with her chair. His gaze landed on her delicious lips as they moved ever so slightly, perhaps in time with her thoughts.

"Better to have your enemy at your side than face one you don't know." Her words were barely a murmur.

He furrowed his brow. Was she giving herself some sort of pep talk? "I'm not your enemy," he said, setting her straight.

Her head snapped around, and she rolled her eyes. "Sorry. I didn't know I said that out loud."

"It's okay."

"Since you did get me into this—" She paused as a wave of uncertainty crossed her face "—yes, I'd appreciate it if you'd escort me home."

Camille watched the shadows as they walked along. Nathaniel was the perfect vampire gentleman, all dark and dangerous, as they strolled down the street. He acknowledged the tourists as they passed and flashed a bit of fang for their benefit.

"I could get used to this," he admitted as one woman jumped away from him. "To think these people come here to be scared."

"I know," she said on a laugh. "Who knew."

"The town is obviously doing well."

They turned down Crossbones Drive, and she stopped in front of the Apex, the town's newest apartment complex. She'd been one of the first residents to move in last year.

"Well, here we are," she told him. "Home sweet home. Thanks."

His eyes raked over her in a way that made her tingle all over. She suddenly felt a strong pull of attraction and wanted to rub up against him like the feline she was.

Oh geez.

She backed away and waved. "See you around."

Holy shuffle-step, that was so lame.

"See you tomorrow," he said in a low voice as she dipped inside the apartment.

Tomorrow? She stood perfectly still, resisting the urge to ease the curtain aside and watch his retreat. No, she would remain strong.

Tilly, her dark tiger tabby cat, and Trouble, her red Maine Coon, walked around her, taking turns zigzagging between her legs as she strolled to the kitchen. "I know. It's been a weird night," she said to them. She grabbed a bottle of water from the refrigerator and gave them each a treat at the same time. "How about for you?"

The animals lumbered into the bedroom alongside her, and she dropped onto the mattress without so much as pulling down the bedspread. Trouble jumped up and pushed her head beneath Camille's hand.

"I think I like the vampire," she said in a sleepy whisper. "But Papa always warned me that they were shady, not to be trusted." She scratched the spot between Trouble's ears, which the cat had strategically placed beneath Camille's fingers. "How is that possible for a Nahuel?"

Nathaniel found an unlocked minivan parked along the street and folded his large form into the backseat. He flicked the lever to recline. It was the closest thing to comfort he could find while still being able to watch Camille's place. Experience told him that if he watched and waited, his bounty would eventually come to him. Either Grey would seek out Camille because the vampire thought she'd wronged him, or he'd pursue Nathaniel because the vamp thought he could eliminate his hunter.

No matter what, Grey was in foreign territory. Nathaniel's number-one concern flitted through his head: what would Grey do when he needed to feed?

As dawn approached, he observed the town closing up shop. The dead of night was the prime time for most supernaturals. He'd noticed some of the stores opened at noon, which made sense. If the tourists got into the paranormal activities, then they'd sleep as late as the townspeople did.

With a groan, Nathaniel got out of the van. He gave Camille's apartment one final glance and then traced to the D&B.

5

Camille rolled out of bed and peered at the clock. *Ugh!* She couldn't believe her eyes. It was two in the afternoon! How could she have slept so late? She stared at the unset alarm clock in disbelief. Now half the things she'd had on her schedule for today weren't going to get done. Great.

Stretching, she padded into the kitchen to the rhythm of a pounding headache. If she didn't know better, she'd think she was hungover. But she'd only had two drinks. Though they had been pretty strong... Her thoughts churned over last night's events, and she gave a groan when she came to the memory of eating ice cream with a sexy vampire.

She paused mid-thought. Did she really think he was sexy? He certainly had a sensual mysteriousness about him...

With an inner feline growl, she had to admit that she was attracted to him. Somehow, she was disappointed in herself for it, though.

"Not one of my better evenings," she told Tibby as the cat jumped onto the table to look out the window.

Camille heated a frozen waffle and ate it on her way to take a shower. It didn't taste very good, but she wasn't in the mood to make anything more complex.

By the time she was clean, dressed, and heading out the door, her headache had subsided and she'd pared her to-do list down to only four items. If traffic wasn't too bad, then she should be able to get them all in before going to the studio. She decided to begin with getting her nails done and finish at the drug store. That would give her a path straight across town.

Her mood improved as she went along. When she was exiting the post office—the third task of the afternoon—she glimpsed Nathaniel across the street at the police station speaking to Alex. Instinctively, she ducked into the shadows and waited until the men left. Had he found the vampire he was after?

It was none of her business, she reminded herself, and moved on to her final task. The promise of teaching class—the dancing and the music—made her feel alive, as it always did.

She had a skip to her step as she unlocked and entered the studio.

This evening's class was the third and final brush-up class scheduled before the Mardi Gras Ball tomorrow night. The residents really got into their activities, and the events were great for her business.

Camille opened the curtains. She'd found that if people could see the dancing, it also helped bring in more customers.

Tonight's group filed in right on time. The conversation among them centered around tomorrow's ball. There was a bit of controversy due to the addition of the Mardi Gras Ball to the Nocturne Fall's calendar since the town council's purists wanted to hold only one monthly event and they'd already had the Valentine's Day Bake-Off. However, the town was expanding now that a lot of younger supernaturals and active families, who wanted things to do, were coming to town.

Camille glanced around the room with a keen eye. It was time to begin, and they were missing folks. "Where are Alex and Hank?"

"They were called to a case," Julian replied. "And Ivy didn't want to come without Hank."

"I heard someone died," a young woman named Sarah added, touching her throat with trembling fingers, as if she was imagining a murderer twisting her neck.

Camille's curiosity rose as the memory of Alex

and Nathaniel talking together earlier flashed in her mind.

Julian thrust his hands into his pockets. "Speaking as VOD, I'm sure we'll hear some news by midnight."

Everyone nodded. There was nothing more to say.

"Okay, let's pair off," Camille told the class.

When they were ready to begin, she stood apart from the group, as she usually did when there was an even number of students. Unexpectedly, the studio door opened. All heads turned to see who had entered, and in the doorway stood Nathaniel Newburg, handsome as ever.

It took her a moment to regain her composure at the sight of him. "If you come in, you dance. Studio rules." She tried to inject some lightness into her tone, anything that wouldn't give away her reaction to him.

Her heart leaped in her chest as he nodded and said, "Okay."

Crap. Honestly, she hadn't thought he'd agree and would just leave. But now that she knew he wasn't going anywhere, she motioned him to the front. "Since everyone is already set, you'll dance with me."

Oh, the warring feelings in her tummy. On one hand, she was quite attracted to him; on the other, he was a vampire. Ugh, why had she insisted he dance?

When he stood across from her, he bowed slightly in acknowledgment.

"Will we be alternating partners?" Julian asked.

"No," Nathaniel said in an adamant tone, not taking his eyes off her.

Camille cleared her throat. "That's not for you to say. However, since tonight we're practicing the tango, which can be complicated, we will remain with the same partners throughout the evening."

Julian made a huffy sound, visibly irritated, but said nothing.

"Okay. The tango." She faced Nathaniel and lifted a hand for him to take. He stunned her by placing his hands in the correct positions. "You've done this before," she whispered.

He smirked. "You don't live several hundreds of years without learning a thing or two."

She rolled her eyes and went on, speaking to the class now. "If you recall, you can dance open, with a bit of space between you, or—" she inched closer until her chest barely touched Nathaniel's, their clothes kissing "—closed, standing almost touching."

He spoke softly, his breath fanning her cheek. "Mmm, I like this."

Me too, she thought but didn't dare say aloud.

They accomplished an eight-count sequence, and hot desire circled down into her hips.

"Find a position with your partner, and let's walk," she instructed the class.

She indicated for Nathaniel to move clockwise around the room. "The male leads, and the woman follows. Each carries their own weight with every step, but in the purest form, the partners move as one."

She turned the lead completely over to Nathaniel, and he moved her into a series of steps. Their breath shared the same space as he pressed his cheek close to hers. His stubble brushed her skin, exciting her and sending a tingling sensation to her toes.

She swallowed, then said to her students, "It's improvisation at its finest."

As class continued, Camille noticed Julian shooting angry glances at Nathaniel. The hometown vamp wasn't into the dancing this evening at all and was clearly just going through the motions.

When they took a break, Camille queued up the next music selection, and she noticed Julian heading straight for Nathaniel.

"I don't think we've met," she overheard him say. "I'm Julian Ellingham."

"Nathaniel Newburg."

The two shook hands.

"Are you just visiting or looking to stay awhile?" Julian asked.

Nathaniel shrugged. "Haven't decided."

"Is this your first time in Nocturne Falls?"

"Yes. I'm from Terror, Minnesota."

Julian pulled himself taller. "I've heard of Terror. Things get pretty intense up there."

"They do," was all Nathaniel said in response.

Camille returned to them. This was a new side of Julian, something beyond the VOD personality she usually saw. He had an edge to him tonight—what she'd call active vampire-mode. Of course, she'd didn't make it a point to hang around the vamp crowd so maybe that wasn't the best way to think of it, but whatever. The two vampires seemed ready to butt chests or something.

"Hey, cool it," she whispered to them, even though she knew everyone in the room could hear. Then she addressed the group at a normal volume. "Okay. One last dance and we're finished for tonight."

Nathaniel spun to glare out the window. "I'll sit this one out," he said, making a beeline for the door.

Confused by his rapid departure and peeved because she wasn't in the position to address the issue while in the middle of class, she let the music play. "Positions," she announced, as the introductory phrase finished.

As the students danced, she couldn't believe how long three minutes could seem. She was itching to find out where Nathaniel had gone. What had she missed?

Outside, Nathaniel exhaled a harsh breath. He'd fled the room for two reasons. First of all, dancing that tango with Camille again would have killed him with desire. His body grew hot with every shift of her hips and undulation of her body. His attraction to her was undeniable, and yet he had no business thinking of her in those seductive terms. He had a traitor to catch and return to Terror. She had a home here, and based on the little he'd gleaned from her, he didn't want to be the one to uproot her.

Secondly, he had caught a hint of conversation outside as two males approached the studio. He began to move toward them. As he got closer, he confirmed his suspicion from the comments he'd overheard: they were the law enforcement officers in Nocturne Falls.

Nathaniel approached cautiously, introducing himself as a bounty hunter and handing the alpha his card.

"I'm Sheriff Hank Merrow," the older man said. "And this is Deputy Cruz."

"Ah yes, we've met." He nodded to Alex. "But I'm pleased to meet your acquaintance, Sheriff." Nathaniel paused. "You're heading to the dance studio?"

"Yes," the sheriff said. "We've had some trouble in town with some visitors, and after questioning Caroline Linzer, we think Camille may have seen our suspect."

"Did Caroline see him?" Nathaniel asked, even though he didn't know who Caroline was. He gathered she was a friend of Camille's.

"No," Merrow replied.

Nathaniel ran his hand over his jaw, looking over his shoulder to the studio. The music had stopped, so class was over. "Look. How about waiting until the students clear out, and then we can all chat?"

Merrow look to Alex, and Alex nodded.

"All right. Fair enough," the sheriff said.

Nathaniel allowed the two men to lead the way. He entered the studio after them and stood off to the side as they sought out Camille.

"We missed you," Sarah said as Hank and Alex walked in.

Alex folded his arms in front of him. "Had a few things to take care of."

"We just stopped by to tell everyone we're looking forward to the ball on Friday," Hank said.

"That's it? You're not going to tell us more?" Julian inquired, still seeming out of sorts.

"Can't. But we will when we know something for certain. We may have an announcement for the news later tonight." Hank's tone indicated he wouldn't be pushed further.

Slowly, the group began to file out. As they left, the conversation among the ladies turned to what they were going to wear to the ball. The men, however, were not happy that the sheriff was keeping secrets. Even if it was a matter of confidentiality, their personalities demanded to be included.

The door closed after everyone except Hank, Alex, and Nathaniel was gone. Camille turned worried eyes to Hank and Alex.

"We wanted to speak to you in private," Alex said, his voice reassuring as he stepped closer to her. He took her hand and held it in his.

The flare of jealousy struck Nathaniel from out of nowhere. He hadn't anticipated feeling so much for her. Heck, he hadn't expected to feel *anything*.

He braced himself for more as her exotic dark-brown eyes widened.

"Is something the matter?" she asked. "You're scaring me."

She remembered the day two years ago when deputies knocked on her door and announced that her parents had been struck and killed by a runaway truck. What she'd learned later was that her parents had been fleeing a vampire. And it was so much more than an unfortunate accident.

Her father had kept a diary where he documented a feud that had started centuries ago between the vampire coven and the feline clan. It had begun with an elopement of a Nahuel with a vampire. Family members on both sides were killed, and the hatred had been passed from one generation to the next.

She could see how such hatred survived. Even now, the trauma from her parents' deaths was still raw.

"We've had a couple of incidents today," Hank started. "And Caroline told us you had something unusual happen last night."

Her gaze slid to Nathaniel and back.

"Let me explain," he said, "since I was the one who dragged you into this." He faced the officers but focused on Hank. "As I told Deputy Cruz earlier, I'm a bounty hunter. I followed a rogue vampire into Nocturne Falls last night, and I lost him somewhere near the studio. That's when I met Camille. Then last night, when Camille was out with her friend, she saw my mark, Payton Grey. I had given her my card so she called me. That's the extent of her involvement."

Hank and Alex exchange a knowing look. "Well, it appears your mark has gone berserk. Someone broke into Creepy Critter Pets last night."

Camille reached over and grabbed Nathaniel's arm for support. Caroline's family owned that store. "No," she gasped.

"Caroline is all right," Alex rushed on. "But the perp killed a few rabbits, and…" He paused.

"We found a dead human near the road into town," the sheriff finished. "We think he was a hitchhiker."

"Oh no!" Her hand flew to cover her mouth, and the jaguar awoke at the intense pain shooting through her chest.

"What can I do to help?" Nathaniel asked.

The sheriff shook his head. "Help us catch him. And then get him out of here."

"That's the plan," Nathaniel said with a nod.

Camille took a long, slow breath, trying to calm her jaguar. "I should go be with Caroline. She's no doubt shaken."

"Yes. As expected," Alex confirmed.

As the sheriff and Nathaniel began to discuss strategy, Alex drew her to the side. "Camille, I want you to be careful. Something is up with this vampire. He's dangerous and unpredictable."

Nathaniel had said the same thing. She swallowed a lump in her throat. "I'll keep a sharp eye out for him."

But even if she encountered this Payton Grey, she had no idea of how to handle him.

6

Sheriff Merrow gave them a lift over to Creepy Critter Pets. Camille was the first one through the door.

"CC!" she called. "Are you all right?"

CC—who Nathaniel gathered was also Caroline—stood up from behind the counter. Camille rushed over to her, and the friends hugged for a long time.

"It was awful," CC said. "Someone broke in. Things were a mess. They let all the animals out of their kennels. And the rabbits..." She burst into tears.

With more calm than she'd displayed at the studio, Camille stroked CC's head. "I'm so sorry."

"I feel so violated," CC said.

"I know."

With a lift of his brow and nod of his chin,

Merrow silently signaled for Nathaniel and Alex to follow him. They went out the back door.

"We found the rabbits out here," Merrow explained. "Although, according to Caroline, they had originally been inside."

Nathaniel flexed his jaw, grinding his molars. "Grey must have a thing for rabbits. He took one on the journey here also. My best guess is that he needed to feed, but the rabbits must not have been enough, so he stumbled across the human and attacked. Some vamps get the short end of the stick when it comes to control."

Merrow nodded. "I don't like that he chose to come to Caroline's place when she was with Camille last night, especially after their run-in with him at Howler's. It doesn't seem like a coincidence to me. What do you think?" He looked at his deputy.

Alex frowned. "Hard to say."

The sheriff sighed and led the way back into the pet shop. With Camille's help, the females had straightened the toppled cans of animal food and were well on the way to having the shop fixed up again.

"Maybe you should stay at my place tonight," Camille suggested to CC.

CC gave a half smile. "That would be nice."

The males helped with some final clean up as CC gathered her things, and then they all exited the shop together.

"Let's hope we catch this vamp before tomorrow evening," Alex said. "We don't want him ruining our ball. I've worked too hard learning those fancy steps." He grinned at Camille, and her face flushed with color.

Nathaniel curled his hands into fists, jealousy raging through him. "Why don't I escort the women home?" he suggested as calmly as he could.

"Good idea," said the sheriff. "Be in touch if you see or hear anything else regarding this vampire, and we'll do the same."

Nathaniel nodded and then guided Camille and CC down the street.

When they reached Camille's doorstep, CC went on inside while Camille lingered with the door ajar. *The poor girl,* he thought of CC. She seemed absolutely spent, and Nathaniel wouldn't be surprised if she was asleep on the couch within minutes.

He gazed at Camille as she pushed her hair away from her face and stretched. Anxiety wound through him as he warred with the decision of what to do next. Should he go back to the D&B, or should he offer to stay?

"I didn't get a chance to tell you earlier," she said, "but you did great dancing tonight."

He smiled. "Thanks."

She wet her lips, staring up at him. "Will you be going to the ball tomorrow night?"

"I haven't decided."

Nodding slowly, she rubbed her neck. "This is such a mess. What this vampire is doing..." She paused, inhaling as if searching for some composure. "I'll admit I'm a little scared."

He didn't think the words came easy for her, and he was honored that she trusted him with this vulnerable side of her. He stepped closer and drew her into a hug. He felt the tension leave her body as she sighed against his chest.

"It will be okay," he said. "I'll handle it."

"What are you going to do?" she asked.

"My job."

She tilted her head back, her brow bunching. "You'll catch him?"

"One way or another." He leaned closer, and before he could think better of it, he gently kissed her brow and then smoothed his lips over her hairline. "I promise," he whispered, his mouth still against her delicate skin.

She turned her head and let her lips brush his ever so lightly.

"You have my phone number. If Grey shows up, call me right away," he said. "I'll check back here throughout the night, though, okay?"

She nodded. Then she stepped away from him and toward the door. Looking over her shoulder, a purring sound escaped her throat. "By the way," she said, "I want to tango tomorrow night. Be ready."

She stepped inside, closing the door behind her.

For a moment, he stood there, frozen in place, his heart hammering, his senses burning for her. No female had made him feel so alive before. Ever. One had never made him anticipate and long for a freaking dance, either.

Finally, he turned and walked away from her apartment, forcing his thoughts back to the case. If he were Payton Grey, where would he be?

Hiding in plain sight.

Yes, he would canvas the town, beginning with a shop where he could pick up something to wear to the ball tomorrow. If he zigzagged across town, perhaps he'd catch the veakling's scent. It was a long shot, but better than waiting around doing nothing.

As it was, finding an appropriate suit turned out to be the easy part. There had been no hint of Grey during his initial canvassing, so he dropped his new three-piece suit off at the D&B where he grabbed his rifle and downed some dinner before setting out again.

For the remainder of the night, he power-traced around town—beginning with the kill spot from the previous evening—looking, assessing, and discarding. Between every other stop, he'd trace to Camille's apartment, just to make sure she and CC were all right.

Exhaustion claimed him at daylight.

*I'll just rest for an hour or so…*he promised himself as he fell into bed.

7

A loud bang sounded, like a door slamming. He shot straight up and sprang from the bed, brandishing one of his deadly handmade knives, his eyes searching the room.

As he got his bearings, he glanced at the bedside clock: *11:00 a.m.*

Man, he was tired. All that tracing last night had taken its toll.

But now that he was awake and listening, the town seemed to be livelier than usual before noon. He reminded himself that not everyone in Nocturne Falls required the cover of darkness that vampires did, but still.

Knowing he wouldn't be able to fall back to sleep, he showered and dressed for the ball early. There were ways around the sunlight problem, and it didn't affect him much to begin with, at least not for brief exposures.

He wore black pants and a button-down beneath his new vest and jacket of large-print, gold-and-red-leaf brocade set against a black background. The look was complemented by a cross pendant of brushed gold. It messed with people's minds for a vampire to wear a cross, but the tale was a myth anyway.

Then he put on gloves, a hat, and sunglasses for added protection during the quick dashes he'd make between buildings, and finally, he slung his rifle over his shoulder.

Always be prepared.

Stepping out from the shadows of the D&B, he hugged the buildings as he traced his way across town. He ducked inside Mummy's Diner and grabbed a seat by the window, shaded by a huge oak tree, where he could watch the foot traffic while he got a cup of coffee. He grinned at the tagline on the menu: *Our food is to die for.*

He placed his coffee order and then rested his elbows on the table, staring out the window. "Where are you, Grey?" he mumbled under his breath.

His gaze skimmed the edges of the street. When he hunted someone, he usually managed to get them to turn and fight, but that wasn't the case this time. Then again, something seemed particularly wrong with this vampire. He preyed on the weak and helpless, even more so than a typical veakling.

Immediately, Nathaniel's mind turned to Camille and CC, and the poor man who had been killed. Vampires didn't have to go after humans. For hundreds of years, there had been manufactured ways feed, so attacking a human like that was a choice.

The sudden thought of Camille falling victim to the likes of Payton Grey created a raging need in his soul, the need to protect her, to love her, to experience everything about her.

But first he had a job to finish.

Camille threw her head back and laughed as the music began. She was in her element, sheer joy oozing from every pore as she danced with several of the students from class.

The decorating committee had outdone themselves. Colorful swaths of fabric in hues of gold, teal, and purple were draped overhead and lit by spotlights. The musicians were outstanding, too. Then there were the attendees, who were dressed in outlandish costumes—a fan of feathers worn as a framed collar, an angelic starburst attached to the back of a dress, a mask of three horns. Most attendees sported masks of some sort actually. Everything was perfect.

Even as she danced, Camille wondered if she could draw Nathaniel to the dance floor. He had shown himself to be surprisingly skilled during class, and she wanted to take another turn with him.

Nathaniel sucked in a breath as he watched Camille dominate the dance floor with her current partner, Alex Cruz, and glared. He *definitely* didn't like those hands touching any part of Camille, nor the smitten look in the guy's eyes. In fact, he had the burning desire to rip the shifter's arms off.

He closed his eyes for a moment, trying to calm himself. When he opened them again, they immediately went to Camille. The teal dress she was wearing shimmered like crystals, but it wasn't nearly as radiant as her smile. From across the room, her gaze kept flicking in his direction, as if she was keeping tabs on him, too.

The refrain died away, and she headed for him. Her eyes met his, challenging and beguiling at the same time.

"I'm glad you came," she said.

He shrugged, trying to hide his attraction as the musical intro of the next piece foretold a tango.

She raised an eyebrow. "So are you going to ask me?"

"What?"

"Don't be so hardheaded," she said with a laugh. "Dance with me."

He hesitated.

"Before the song is over," she prompted.

His feet moved toward her, his heart following her request without his mind's permission.

They walked toward the dance floor together, and when they got to where Alex now stood, she said, "Let him hold the gun."

It took a moment for her request to register. He was so into her that he'd completely forgotten the rifle still slung over his shoulder. Since Alex was a deputy, Nathaniel didn't hesitate to hand him the weapon.

Then, in the center of the dance floor, despite the fact that she'd more or less dragged him out there, he assumed the lead.

Her heart sped up, thumping against her breast as he slid an arm around her and drew her to him. She stepped into his shadow, and he wheeled her around like a tree branch in a storm. In a totally improvisational dance of seduction, she circled her foot to one side and tapped it behind the other. She existed on the balls of her feet, ready to move at his direction. Her chest pressed against his, their thighs brushing—a sacred connection as his step opened and closed in an effortless glide across the floor. She reached her hand up the back of his neck and caressed his nape, resting her cheek against his.

In this moment, she was his partner, his lover…his everything. He created a space, and she entered it of her own violation, then twisted her hips left and right. It felt like they were the only two beings in the room as everything else fell away. He was walking a tightrope and taking her along with him. It was a unique communication between a vampire and a shifter, and with his command and precision, she felt worshiped and alive.

When the music ended, they both were nearly panting, their breath mingling. Nathaniel looked deeply into her eyes. "We will continue this later," he murmured hoarsely.

Her lungs grappled for air as she inhaled a long, steadying breath. "I'd like that."

He didn't touch her as he escorted her off the floor. He'd done enough of that. Every part of his body was singing to know her more intimately, and yet he knew it wasn't a good idea. His place was back in Terror; her life was here.

"Fresh air?" he asked.

"Absolutely."

They made their way past the stares of the people in this close-knit community and out into the cool February night. He vaguely heard the emcee announce that it was time to meet the Mardi Gras king and queen, Hugh and Delaney Ellingham.

"Would you like something to drink?" Nathaniel asked Camille, realizing he should've offered her one before they'd gone outside.

"Yes, that would be wonderful." She fanned her face. He noticed the flush of jaguar spots glistening on her skin. She was absolutely beautiful.

"I'll be right back," he promised, then left her there, leaning against the entrance railing.

As he was filling his second glass of punch, movement caught his eye at the end of the serving table. He didn't have to lift his head to know who it was. His brother's scent rushed to him on the Georgia breeze. The wheelchair inched forward as their gazes collided, full of emotions neither of them wanted to release.

Nathaniel slowly stepped toward Jake. After all these years, Nathaniel still wasn't ready to make amends. That would mean accepting Jake's forgiveness. No, he didn't deserve Jake's forgiveness.

Suddenly, a scream sliced through the air. It had sounded like it had come from outside, and his eyes widened.

Camille!

He dropped the punch glass onto the table, the red liquid spilling all over. Running—there were too many people around to risk tracing—he shoved his way through the crowd. But when he got to where he'd left her, she was gone. Only her scent remained...and that of Payton Grey.

8

Anger filled Nathaniel. How could he have let his guard down like that? He slammed his fist on the railing as Alex appeared and tossed the rifle to him. He caught it mid-stride as he tried to follow the scents—one clearly vampire, one delicately female. But there were too many people. Plus, the breeze alone was strong enough to dilute their odors.

Damn.

"He has Camille," Nathaniel bit out.

"I heard her scream and figured there was trouble," Alex said.

Jake rolled to a stop behind them. "I see you're still in the same line of work."

Nathaniel scowled. "How could I not be?"

"Did you see which way he took her?" Alex asked, glancing between the two vampires.

"No," Nathaniel growled.

The crowd inside cheered and clapped, drowning out their conversation, most of the attendees not even noticing that anything was awry.

Sheriff Merrow burst out into the night. "Split up," he ordered.

Nathaniel agreed. They would cover more ground by moving in different directions. He followed Camille's strong, fearful scent.

"Grey doesn't have much of a lead on us," he called over his shoulder. "And since he's dragging Camille along with him, he probably won't trace."

"So sure of yourself, aren't you, little brother?" Jake asked after him.

"When I'm finished with this case, we're going to talk," Nathaniel vowed.

Jake said nothing as his brother left him behind.

When Nathaniel reached the gargoyle fountain, he spotted Grey as the vamp shoved Camille into the driver's seat of a beautiful old Corvette and then climbed in the other side.

"Drive." The rogue vampire's order came to Nathaniel on the wind.

Camille fumbled as she put the car in gear and took off around the fountain. Just as she entered the straightaway of Black Cat Boulevard, he raised his rifle, sighted it, and shot the rear tire of the Corvette, praying she'd still be able to control the car as it slowed.

The vehicle immediately skidded to a stop. His heart pounded in his ears, making it difficult to hear anything, even with his heightened senses. The car door opened, and Camille barreled free from the car, running down the street toward him.

Grey slid into the driver's seat and put the car back in motion. Despite the deflated tire, he gunned it, heading straight for Camille.

The bastard was going to run her down.

Nathaniel traced to push her out of the way, but before he reached her, she had transformed into a sleek, powerful jaguar and jumped into the air, clearing a vehicle parked along the street and landing on all fours at the doorstep of the Hallowed Bean.

He ended the trace on the sidewalk as she shifted back into her human form. Nathaniel stood there, somewhat in shock, when he saw that Camille was unharmed.

The Corvette spun in a circle then, coming to rest sideways across the street.

Nathaniel traced over to it and ripped open the driver's door. He dragged Grey out of the car, then jerked back his fist. "Sink your teeth into this, pretty boy." He punched the vamp in the face. He was so angry he could have killed him, right then and there. Camille could have been seriously injured or worse.

Inhaling a rugged breath, he hauled Grey's hands

behind him and secured them with handcuffs.

The sheriff and deputy ran up to them. "We heard the shot," Merrow said. "Is everyone okay?"

Nathaniel nodded. "Yeah. I just took out a tire."

"Nice going," Alex said. He moved to clap Nathaniel on the shoulder but stopped, seeming to think better of the idea.

"Can you hold him until tomorrow?" Nathaniel asked Merrow. "Then I'll take him back to Terror."

The sheriff nodded. "Sure. We have a cell especially for vampires."

"Good," he said, walking away. "I need to take care of something."

He rushed over to Camille. With her back plastered against the café window, she didn't even turn her gaze to look at him. She stared at the car that had nearly struck her.

"Cami?" The nickname rolled from his lips without thought.

She snapped her head toward him. "Don't. That's what my dad used to call me."

"Are you hurt?" he asked, ignoring her comment in favor of making sure she was all right.

Her hand moved to the center of her chest. "That's exactly how my parents died—run down by a crazy vampire." Her voice wobbled, full of disbelief.

He didn't quite understand what she was talking about, but he also sensed now wasn't the time to press her about it. Her gaze turned up and met his. He could see the confusion in her eyes, hear the swish of air as she inhaled and exhaled in a struggle to calm herself.

"Thank you," she whispered.

He drew her into a hug, tugging her into his chest. At first she tensed, resisting, then she relaxed and melted into him on a sigh. After a minute or two, he asked, "Can you walk?"

She pushed off him and blinked. "Of course I can." With a twirl of her dress, she stepped away from the window to prove it.

Her sass was back, and he fought a grin. He was never going to understand felines. "Good. Would you like to return to the ball or grab a cup of coffee?"

She smiled wickedly. "How about we go to my place and pick up the tango where we left off?"

He held out a hand for her to take. "I do so love that dance."

Want more?
The story moves to Terror, Minnesota as it continues in Larissa Emerald's Blood Keepers series. Watch for the next episode in FOREVER AT RISK.

The Shaman Charms the Shifter
A Nocturne Falls Universe Story

Leopard shifter Sasha Weisberg arrives in Nocturne Falls hoping someone in the town of supernaturals might be able to undo the spell an angry ex-friend put on her. Otherwise, she's doomed to live most of every day as a bird, with only three precious hours each day to enjoy her human form and her snow leopard not at all.

An archangel friend convinces Kianso Kane to travel to Nocturne Falls for a weekend of rest and relaxation. From the onset of the trip, his shaman calling challenged him to return to his Hawaiian roots and acknowledged his shaman birthright. His instincts led him right to Sasha and he knew straightaway she was his true love. But she was caught in a maelstrom of a witches curse. And until she was free, she couldn't be completely his.

They have one chance on Samhain to undo the curse, or else her next chance won't be for nineteen years. Can she trust Kianso and his visions?

1

Kianso Oka Kane glanced at Seth in the stylist's mirror as the archangel strolled through the entrance and into the salon's waiting area. He tucked his wings tight against his back and out of sight from human eyes. Otherwise, he probably would have knocked over the nearby product display case.

"Howzit, brah?" Kianso said.

Seth halted and leaned one shoulder against the wall with his arms crossed over his chest. "Hey, Five-O. You want to find some action this weekend? I'm heading to Nocturne Falls. Want to come with?"

"Trim over the ears a bit shorter, please," he said to the stylist, then moved his gaze to Seth. The archangel had nicknamed him after the *Hawaii*

Five-O TV show. Hearing it always made him smile. There were worse things to be associated with.

"Well?" Seth asked, his lack of patience getting the best of him.

"I know it's not far, but I've never been to Nocturne Falls," Kianso said. "What's it like?"

The stylist piped up, her Georgia accent just as sweet as it could be. "It's super awesome. My man and I went a few months ago. The town celebrates Halloween all year long, and the townspeople dress up every day. Vampires, werewolves, and other paranormal creatures roam the streets. You should go. It's fun."

"I can't believe you've never been, man. It's like an hour and a half from Tyler."

Kianso shrugged. "I'm happy being a small-town lawyer. I have no desire to gallivant around."

It was true. He was like a general practitioner: his practice handled estate planning, tax law, family law, personal injury, and bankruptcy, just to name a few. He did everything except criminal law. In Georgia, 70 percent of the lawyers worked out of Atlanta, but he had not wanted to run that big-city rat race. The desire for a more laid-back lifestyle was the one thing he took with him when he left Hawaii. Tyler, Georgia, gave him that. Life was good, even if a little lonely at times.

"Come on. It's the weekend," Seth pressed. "Let's go chill for a while. Venn and his bride have returned from France, and the Divine Tree is back under his protection. I'm finally free. And I'm ready to let loose a little before the next Guardian calls me with some dire dilemma." He rolled his eyes.

"You should get that mop of yours trimmed, old man," Kianso said, evading the question at hand. He eyed Seth's head of dreads. The archangel reminded him more of Jack Sparrow in that pirate movie than an angelic being. Not that he understood such things. But his shaman side knew there were paranormal creatures in this world. That's probably why his best friend was the shape-shifting Divine Tree Guardian Venn Hearst. Yep, there were unexplainable creatures in this world, like the ones who protected special trees against evil and demons, and… Well, and more things he didn't want to think about.

The stylist brushed the loose hair from around his neck and then removed the drape. Kianso slipped his glasses into place. He stood and reached into his pocket to grab the bills he already had ready. "Thanks," he said, passing the tip to the petite woman. "Looks great. See you in a couple of weeks."

Given his Hawaiian heritage, his hair grew thick, and it required frequent trimming to maintain the business look he liked. As he headed for the door, Seth fell into step beside him. They exited onto the street.

"Well?" Seth asked again.

Kianso kept walking. It was Columbus Day weekend. He didn't have to meet with clients until Tuesday afternoon. But did he really want to visit a town that celebrated Halloween 365 days a year? Hell, yeah. He couldn't believe he hadn't been to the spooky town already.

From the other side of the street, a bird flew across his path—a red-tailed hawk. He stepped sideways as it zoomed past. Kianso stopped short. As a spirit animal, the hawk was powerful and unrelenting, presenting messages of courage, wisdom, and illumination from the universe, prodding him to see the bigger pictures of truth and experience—the wise use of opportunities, magic, and focus, and how to overcome problems.

He felt the light press of a hand on his shoulder. It seemed to give him a slight shove toward Seth. It was his sister, Jen. The strong essence of her spirit floated all around him. She had died in a mudslide eight years ago along with their parents. And even though he missed his *makuahine* and *makuakane*, it was his sister's death that had shattered him, causing him to leave the island.

Out of nowhere, the scent of Play-Doh intertwined in his memory as he recalled growing up with his sister. They'd spent hours sculping animals out of the colorful modeling clay. Creating things with her hands was her favorite pastime. She was an artist…he was the practical one.

And even with the pain of losing her, he was glad they had their time together. She'd had a hand in shaping him into the man he was today. She still did.

After her death, he'd abandoned his shaman training and fled, and now, her spirit urged him as if she were right there with him.

Why couldn't she just let him be?

He peered at the archangel. "She's here, isn't she?" he inquired, wanting confirmation.

Seth's only response was a half smile and a lift of his brow.

Kianso pressed his lips together and then allowed his cheeks to billow slightly as he exhaled. She was telling him it was time he embraced his shamanic heritage. Practically no one knew about that side of him. But he suspected that Seth knew. Even though Kianso had never come out and told the archangel, Seth knew. It was there in his shrewd glance.

Kianso rolled his shoulders and stretched his neck. He *could* use a vacation. "Naw. I should stay at home and work on my knitting."

Seth smiled at Kianso's mischievous glance. "Excellent," the archangel said.

"I'll pick up a few things from my place and then the weekend is ours."

For some reason, the decision to get away didn't excite him as much as it should have.

81

Kianso's brows bunched as a wave of apprehension washed over him. If he took the time to tune in to his shamanic instincts, he might be able to foresee what lay ahead in Nocturne Falls. But no, that wasn't who he was now. He'd turned away from magic years ago; he'd left that part of himself back in Hawaii. It had failed him then, and it would fail him now. He no longer trusted what he couldn't see and touch.

So with a firm sense of control over his future, he resisted the tug to heed his shamanic voice, struggling against the feeling of expectation and urgency.

Both men slid into his royal-blue Mustang convertible, and he drove away from the quaint shops of downtown Tyler.

When he got to his apartment building, which sat on the edge of a private golf course, he cut the car's engine. "You wanna come up?" he asked as he got out.

Seth locked his hands behind his head and leaned back. "No, thanks. I'll just soak up some sun while you're gone. You never know when the first cold snap will appear. Better enjoy it while I can."

"Huh. You won't be here by then anyway." Kianso dashed into the lobby before Seth could respond and took the elevator up to the fourth floor. He unbuttoned his dress shirt at the neck and removed his tie. He peered out a large, paned window as he made his way from the living room into the bedroom. Outside, a hawk soared in a flight pattern above the trees—his spirit animal guide. He'd seen it various times in his life since his sister's passing.

No. He tightened his jaw and spun away from the window.

Flipping through his closet, he tossed jeans and a couple of shirts into a satchel. He didn't imagine Nocturne Falls was much different from Tyler, so he didn't think he'd need anything special to wear. Most Georgia towns looked the same, all having a similar Southern charm.

Several minutes later, he landed back in the driver's seat and fired up his GPS. "Directions to Nocturne Falls," he said aloud.

As he drove away, he thought he heard the hawk squawk its approval.

In the yard behind Creepy Critter Pets, Sasha perched on a sturdy branch overlooking the patio. Living in the body of a bird sucked...big-time. She was a gorgeous green Quaker parrot. Her face, neck, and chest were pale gray, her back and tail feathers gleamed a green to yellow, and her wing feathers contrasted in blue. But still...a bird. For crying out loud, she ate birds when in her shape-shifter cat form. Now, all because a witch got her britches twisted, she was wearing feathers almost full time.

Sheesh. She inhaled a calming breath. She had faith that she would find a way out of the curse Lilly Reese had put on her. *Just stay positive and the answer will come.*

Above her, a flock of cardinals battled three ravens, trying to outdo one another in song. The noise made Sasha grin. Even though she couldn't actually credit the ravens as singing—their voices sounded more like squawks—they were so filled with life and vigor as their voices carried on the cool October breeze. She wished she felt such abandon.

Caroline Linzer, a longtime friend and the pet store owner, strolled out carrying a fragrant cup of coffee and settled in a chair at the patio table. A hint of envy twisted in Sasha. How she'd love a cup of joe right now.

Caroline glanced up into the trees and squinted through heavy-lidded eyes, then lifted her coffee cup to her lips and drank. Her friend murmured a pleased sound. It was her usual late-afternoon cup of joe to help her get through that sleepy time of day.

Sasha wasn't tired, though. In a few minutes, she'd change into her human self. Then the next three hours were the highlight of her day.

"Thank goodness for caffeine," Caroline mumbled.

"CC... CC... CC," Sasha singsonged. It was the nickname she'd learned from Camille, Caroline's friend who had moved to Minnesota earlier this year. Sasha had picked it up during a phone call that Caroline had put on speaker.

"What? Are you trying to outdo the other feathers up there?" Caroline asked, angling her chin toward the other birds.

"Don't insult me," Sasha said in a scrappy bird voice and then dipped her beak into the down beneath one wing and scratched. "I don't give a wit."

Caroline sighed. "Sorry, Sasha. Being caught in a spell must be rough, and I understand happens more often than people think. A witch, warlock, or sorcerer has a disagreement with someone, and *bam!* In their anger and frustration, a spell is cast."

"I know. I know. I just need to up my search for a remedy. There are more supernaturals in Nocturne Falls than anywhere else. Surely one of the residents knows how to undo it and return me to my feline shape-shifter self." Thankfully, she was able to articulate as her human self; however, her speech came out in a birdy voice that really exhausted her patience. She tired of hearing it.

Caroline had been a tremendous help, taking her in, helping her discover the food she needed, being her friend.

At the moment, her life was in limbo. She'd left

Montgomery and given up her job as a recreation supervisor for the city. She hadn't had much choice, really. It was pretty hard to work in bird form, especially when she was stuck like this twenty-one hours of every day.

In the shop, the mantel clock chimed 5:00 p.m. Yes! The change began. Her wings shifted into arms and hands, and she dropped to the floor on legs and feet that absorbed the landing on hard ground. It felt wonderful! She stretched.

It was time for Caroline to lock up. She closed the store at the same time during the week, with short hours on Saturday, finishing at four, and Sundays, when the store didn't open at all. In a town like Nocturne Falls, people liked to dine and drink and play when the sun went down, not shop for pets.

When Caroline finished closing the store, she ambled out back again. Sasha sat at the table in her human form, draining the last sip of coffee from Caroline's cup.

"Sorry," Sasha said impishly. "It's been a long day." She walked the cup past Caroline, into the store, and into the kitchen area where she proceeded to wash it. Caroline joined her. "Let's go. I have a limited time before I change back into that infernal bird. I plan to make the most of every second. If you don't mind, can we visit Misty's Boo-Tique? There was a cute outfit in the window." She licked a final taste of coffee from her lips.

"Flying around makes for terrific window shopping."

Caroline chuckled softly. "Fine with me. Lead the way."

Without hesitation, Sasha did just that, only pausing to let Caroline lock the door behind them.

Sasha's steps quickened. There wasn't a minute to waste. It was extremely frustrating to be trapped for most of the day, only allowed to assume her human form for three hours each day and not being permitted to enjoy her snow leopard form at all.

Sasha lengthened her stride, allowing her legs to stretch, enjoying the tug and pull of her muscles as she strolled down the lane. A bird's legs didn't have the same feel. The difference in anatomy wasn't something she would have contemplated before, but now, well, she was experiencing the contrasts up close and personal. So when she transformed into her human form for those few hours, it was heaven.

It took them around fifteen minutes to walk to Misty's Boo-Tique. The outfit she'd admired this afternoon was on a mannequin in the display window. The window dressing fit the Halloween theme of the town with a timeworn haunted house motif, featuring a lot of spider webs, a huge bird cage suspended from the ceiling, and a few whispy ghosts flying in the background. Sasha pointed to the mannequin on the right seated in a chair. "That coral halter top. Isn't it adorable?"

"Yep. Very cute."

Entering the store, they headed to the clothes racks. Sasha tried on the outfit from the window plus several more. Her heart felt lighter minute by minute as she twisted and turned in front of the mirror along with Caroline. As she paid for her purchases she checked her phone for the time. "OMG, we've spent nearly an hour playing around here."

A breeze fluttered across her cheeks as she stepped outside. She brushed her hair behind one ear. "I feel like fish for dinner tonight," she said, glancing sideways at Caroline. "Do you think Mummy's Diner has that?"

"They should. Maybe tilapia or something, if that's what you're after."

The snow leopard shifter in Sasha was partial to fish. She swept her tongue along her lips. All she'd had today were a handful of seeds and a couple of berries. A delicious seafood dinner was just what she needed. Her stomach growled at the thought.

Caroline grinned. "Oh my. You *are* hungry, aren't you?"

Sasha picked up her pace. Her precious time would go by in a blink. She had been in Nocturne Falls for five days now and had determined that, even though it was a small, quaint town, there were a lot of places she'd like to visit—the winery, Delaney's Delectables, the Illusions jewelry store, to name a few. But with her time limitations, she'd had very little time to check out the town in human form. And moving forward, all her efforts needed to be focused on connecting with the witches of Nocturne Falls. So far, she'd learned that Alice Biship was the most powerful witch, although there seemd to be many reasons why people wouldn't want to approach her. Corette Williams was also a very powerful witch and owned the Ever After bridal boutique in town. She had three daughters: Pandora, a local real estate agent; Charisma, who was a professional life coach; and Marigold, who owned a flower shop. Surely one of them would know how to reverse this confounded spell.

When they reached the entrance to Mummy's Diner, Caroline held the door open for her. Sasha's eyes adjusted quickly to the dim lighting as she entered, her cat instincts taking over. The sign at the entrance advised SEAT YOURSELF, so she headed for the vacant booth in the back where it was quiet and secluded.

Sasha checked her watch. Fixating on the time was becoming a bad habit. She sighed.

The waitress came over with a smile. "Hi. Can I get you something to drink?"

"No, thank you," Sasha replied. "I'm mainly

interested in food." As if on cue, her stomach rumbled again.

The waitress raised a brow. "Okay. We can handle that."

"Caroline?" Sasha asked, finding her manners.

"I'm just going to glance at the menu," she said. "You go ahead."

"I'd like seafood. Any recommendations?" Sasha asked.

"We have a Fish-and Chips special" the waitress told her.

"Perfect."

Caroline set her menu on the table. "I'll have the same, actually, and just some water please."

"Excellent," the waitress said, picking up the menus. "Two Fish-and-Chip specials coming right up."

As the woman walked away, all Sasha could think was, *Hurry*.

2

It was almost seven by the time Kianso pulled into Nocturne Falls. The sun had set, and the automatic street lighting came on as he progressed. He drove down Main Street, noting the orange-and-purple Halloween motif and the jack-o'-lanterns that graced many of the business doorsteps and windows.

"They are really serious about the town's themed moneymaker," he said.

"Hey, Mummy's Diner is up on the right," Seth said, ignoring Kianso's comment. "Pull in there and we'll grab a bite before we go to the condo. I'll restock the fridge tomorrow."

Kianso did as instructed and parked the car. "How often do you come here?" he asked when he joined Seth on the sidewalk. He looked at the archangel, noticing that he didn't fold in his wings the way he usually did. Instead, he let them drape free in all their glory, the shimmery feathers reflecting the twinkling lights along the sidewalk.

"Mummy's or Nocturne Falls?" Seth asked.

"The latter."

"Not often enough. I purchased a condo in the Excelsior right after it was built. Figured it was a good investment and close to Tyler and my duties there. But I've only used it a handful of times. Hopefully, I can visit more this year."

"But the hesitation in your voice says you don't expect to."

Seth shrugged his massive shoulders, causing his wings to move with the motion. "There's a lot of ruthless evil and destruction going on right now. So I won't hold my breath."

Kianso wondered if angels actually breathed. He'd never really paid attention.

"Come on," Seth nudged. "Their Better-Than-Sex Pie is divine."

"Hmph," Kianso grunted. "Guess you have privileged info on that. I mean, you hang out in heaven, right? Can pie be better than that?"

"Maybe one day I'll give you a glimpse."

"I'm in no hurry."

Inside, Seth guided them toward the only empty table left in the place. Thankfully, there was enough space to accommodate his wings. A waiter appeared, barely giving them a chance to glance at the menu in his enthusiasm. Kianso wondered if he was new at the job. He and Seth both ordered Zombie burgers…big bad burgers.

Kianso swept his gaze around the room. There seemed to be a balanced mix of supernatural beings and humans. A troll couple was sitting in the corner booth, a foursome of vampires was at another table, a pair of human women were giggling at a nearby table, and then another set of women were at the booth next to Seth and Kianso.

As he watched the two women nearest to them, the one on the far side of the booth peered across the space at him. Her eyes latched on to him and held. In that moment, he couldn't look away.

Did he know her? A flutter winged through his gut, and as he continued to look at her, her smile grew.

She had intense, deep-blue eyes that didn't blink or waver. Her white-blond hair barely touched her shoulders. She looked stunning in tan pants and a leopard-print top. Who was she? What sort of creature?

A beautiful one, his mind answered.

She was sitting up straight in her seat, her slender neck and head angled toward him. She wore it swept to the side, so he could see her brow pinch slightly before she glanced down and the curtain of hair fell and hid her face.

Look up, he thought. *Look at me.*

She did, tucking a lock of her hair behind one ear with her delicate fingers.

The vibe she was emitting reached out and touched him, curled around him. His energy crashed into hers, and they circled in the space between them. Heat swept through him, settling in his groin as she looked at him from beneath long lashes. He had to learn who she was.

Seth turned his head and followed Kianso's gaze. "She's striking," the archangel said.

"Yes. And there's something going on with her. I can't quite put my finger on it," Kianso admitted. "I just…feel her tension."

At that moment, she glanced at her watch and an anxious expression flitted over her features. She rose quickly, dropped her napkin onto her plate, and dashed past him, practically running out of the diner.

Before Kianso realized what he was doing, he was following her. But when he got to the door and scanned the walk, she wasn't anywhere in sight. *Where did she go?*

He blinked and peered left, then right. *Strange.* The crowd on the street was too light to get lost in. Did she possess magical powers where she could simply disappear?

Frustrated and disappointed, he went back inside Mummy's, where a woman with a riot of red hair stood beside the table speaking to Seth.

The archangel made introductions. "Kianso, this is Pandora Williams, the top real estate agent in Nocturne Falls. She gave me the heads-up when the Excelsior condos were being built."

"Pleasure to meet you," Kianso said, offering his hand.

Her green eyes flashed with enthusiasm. "Likewise. Welcome to Nocturne Falls. What do you think of our little town so far?"

"It's very unusual," he said. "I've only just arrived, so I'm looking forward to the tour tomorrow."

She paused, seeming to assess him with those shrewd emerald eyes. "I'm sure Seth knows all the best places to show you." She looked at Seth. "Don't you, darling?"

Seth grinned. "Absolutely. And they have some of the best food anywhere."

Kianso chuckled softly. "Leave it to him to know where the finest crepe, sushi, or steak is being served." Then he let his gaze slide past Pandora to the table where his mystery woman had been sitting. Her dining companion was still there.

"Pandora, who is that woman?" he asked. Since she seemed to have a finger on the pulse of the town, he figured Pandora may know her.

Pandora twisted around to eye the woman. "Oh. That's Caroline Linzer. She owns Creepy Critter Pets."

His heart began to race. If Pandora knew Caroline, maybe she also knew his mystery woman. "Did you happen to see the blond woman who was with her?" he asked. "She just left."

She frowned. "No, I'm afraid not. Why?"

"Just wondering. She, um, looked familiar," he said, which was true. He simply couldn't recall where he'd seen her before.

Pandora stepped backward, giving him the once-over, then leaned in closer. "You're not a normie, are you?" she whispered. "You're a supernatural."

"Not really," he answered. "Back home in Hawaii, I was a shamanic warrior. But that was a lifetime ago. I've given that up."

"Have you now?" She raised an eyebrow. "Once a witch doctor, always a witch doctor, I always say."

Seth hooted. "You tell him, Pandy."

Kianso straightened and cleared his throat. "Shamans are *not* witch doctors."

Pandora moved in the direction of the door. As she traveled by him, she patted his shoulder. "If you say so." She glanced at Seth and gave a wave. "See you boys around."

Kianso watched her exit and then slid into his chair. Out of the corner of his eye, he noticed Caroline Linzer scurrying after Pandora and catching the witch's attention on the sidewalk outside.

The waiter delivered their food, and Kianso

murmured his thanks. When he glanced out the front window again, the women were gone.

Seth smacked his lips. "I'm starving."

"You're always starving."

"Food is one of the simplest pleasures life has to offer." He lifted the thick, good old-fashioned hamburger from his plate and sunk his teeth into it with a throaty moan.

Kianso paused, admiring the work of art, the plump, pub-style burger with lettuce and tomato and red onions. He took a bite and then dabbed the napkin at his chin as the juices of the burger ran over his stubble. As he ate, he had to admit that the food at Mummy's Diner really was terrific.

"If you like Italian we can eat at Guillermo's tomorrow," Seth said.

"Sounds good to me. Mmm, this is delicious." He ate another bite. "Although, I'm happy to eat Italian food seven days a week, too."

"An Italian-lovin' Hawaiian. Learn something new every day." Seth lifted a shoulder — and wing with it — and then let it fall back into place.

The waitress slid two slices of Better-Than-Sex pie onto the table. Seth raised his fork and waggled his brows in an exaggerated show of anticipation. A forkful of the creamy-chocolaty dessert disappeared into his friend's mouth and he closed his eyes as a satisfied expression washed over his face. He pointed his fork a Kianso. "Try it."

He did. The pie tasted delicious. Even so, his gaze drifted to the next table. There was just something about her he couldn't ignore.

The next thing Kianso knew, his fork was scraping an empty plate. And while the first bites had been fabulous, he couldn't say he'd noticed the rest. He was too fixated on his thoughts of the girl with the white-blond hair. Which seemed odd since one, he didn't usually go for blondes, and two, he wasn't looking for a woman to complete him...and all that romantic gibberish.

3

Sasha only had to fly a short distance to find a place to land. She was breathing hard and her heart beat wildly against her ribs...not due to exertion but because of the way the gorgeous stranger's look had made her feel. Like he desired her. And for those few crazy moments, before she'd had to flee, she'd known an all-consuming need to meet him. How could the sensations of belonging and desire be so intense in such a short time?

Once again, this blasted curse had interfered in her life. Ugh, ruins and rain. She couldn't take this much longer.

Letting go of her immense disappointment, she scanned the area to get her bearings. Her claws tried to grip a substance as hard as rock. She glanced down. Actually, it was rock. She perched on the shoulder of the massive stone gargoyle that adorned the fountain in the center of town.

From the direction of Mummy's, Caroline approached, carrying their shopping bags and talking to a woman with a riot of red hair. They paused a few feet away. She strained to overhear the conversation between them, and learned Caroline was speaking to Pandora, one of the town's witches she sought to interview.

"Pandora, so you see, my friend is looking for someone—another witch—who might be able to undo the spell put on her in the midst of a quarrel."

If Sasha had hands, she would have clapped. Caroline was pleading her case to Pandora Williams, one of the witches in town she'd told her about. Excitement whirled in her chest.

Suddenly, the world began to move, as did the stone beneath her claws. She shifted her weight, but she couldn't find purchase in the stone.

"Get off me," a hard voice grumbled.

Sasha felt as if she was on a roller coaster until she flapped her wings and then resettled. Water splashed about, and then a large stone hand swatted in her direction. "Off, I say."

Whoa! The gargoyles were real creatures, she realized, not merely fixtures!

Another spray of water droplets fell through the air, and Sasha flew to the fountain's edge. Pandora and Caroline both turned their heads and stared at her.

"There she is," Caroline said, brushing wetness from her arm. "Sasha, this is Pandora Williams. She's the witch I told you about."

"Hello," she squawked.

"She doesn't like talking much in bird form," Caroline explained.

Pandora frowned. "Well, fiddlesticks. Then I don't see how I can help you, darling." She turned to leave.

"Wait," Sasha said. "For three hours every evening I'm human again. Maybe we could meet you during that time tomorrow? Between five to eight in the evening. That's when I'm my normal self."

Pandora glanced at Sasha and then back at Caroline. "That's a difficult time. And tomorrow's Saturday. My family always gathers for dinner, and then we have a party to attend."

"The engagement bash Nick is throwing Van and Lisa?" Caroline asked.

"Yes. Are you attending?"

"I am. Sasha, too, granted the timing works out in her favor. Perhaps we can talk a little more then?"

Pandora nodded. "In the meantime, I'll confer with my mother and sisters. Maybe they've had some experience with spells of wrath." She withdrew a business card from the side of her purse and offered it to Caroline.

"Perfect." She accepted the card.

"Thank you," Sasha chirped, gratitude swelling in her chest.

"You're welcome. See you then." As she passed the fountain, Pandora said, "Nick, you may want to go below and dry off."

"A few drops of water never hurt anyone," the gargoyle muttered and struck a different pose.

Sasha was awestruck. She learned something new about Nocturne Falls every day, and it was always something as remarkable as it was strange.

It was after ten that evening when they arrived at Seth's condo.

"Just pull up front," Seth told Kianso. "The valet will park the car."

"Seriously?" Kianso said, surprised at how nice the place was. He craned his neck and looked up at the five-story building as he got out of his Mustang and grabbed his bag out of the trunk. It wasn't the fanciest or largest place he'd ever been, of course. The big cities with their high-rises would surpass it in a minute. But for a small Georgia town, the Excelsior was pretty swanky. All clean lines, accent lights, and modern touches.

He recalled what Seth had said about buying the place as an investment. How many such investments did the archangel have?

They entered a small lobby, and the man at a bell desk waved at Seth. "Good to see you, sir," he said.

"Same here," Seth replied as he led the way to the elevator on the left. Kianso guessed the right one was exclusive to the penthouse, as it was in many luxury buildings like this one. While they waited for their ride up, he noted a fitness room and pool set back behind a classy glass entry off to the right. Too bad he didn't come prepared to use either.

They stepped on the elevator and took it to the fourth floor. When they exited, Kianso immediately discerned a distinct division in occupancy. The space seemed to be divided into two condos, both quite spacious judging from the size of the building.

"I'm to the right." Seth indicated with flick of his hand. "I liked this place because of its security. Since I only come here once in a while, it was perfect, and as I mentioned, close to Tyler."

"It's really nice," Kianso remarked.

Seth smirked. "I think so." He punched in the code of an electronic combination lock beside the door to his condo and entered.

Kianso hung back as the archangel pushed a button on the wall, engaging window shades that lifted to the ceiling. The lights of Nocturne Falls danced below. The place was decked out in an eclectic mix of sleek, modern style and old-world charm. The masculine combination of leather and glass fit Seth well, too.

"Make yourself at home," he instructed. "The guest room is down the hall to the left." He pointed to the corridor he meant.

"Thanks," Kianso said. "I think I'm going to turn in. Dessert put me over the top."

"It was good, huh?"

"Oh yeah." His belly was full to bursting, especially after feasting on the Better-Than-Sex Pie the archangel had insisted Kianso try. Catchy name, and damned good, but better than sex? Well, not in his life. Even though it had been a very, very long time since he'd had anyone in his bed.

After they got settled, Seth went back out. Obviously, the archangel didn't require the sleep Kianso did. He dropped into bed, closed his eyes, and was out.

But in his sleep, he felt his feet moving, walking along a path of some kind. The earth pushed hard against his feet as a mist swirled around him. In some spots, a cool breeze brushed his face; in others, hot, moist air pressed down on him. The path wound through a deep forest, and he followed.

When he approached a bend in the path, he saw an eagle perched on a dead tree stump. "When are you coming home?" the eagle asked, staring straight into his eyes.

Kianso straightened. Part of him tamped down his shamanic voice, while the other part listened. An eagle spirit animal indicated it was time to look inward with a careful eye and to allow the heart to be one's guide.

He stared at the eagle and pressed his lips together. *This is a dream, nothing more.*

So he strolled on.

The trees seemed even taller, even grander in the next stretch of the forest.

He came to another sharp curve in the path where a coyote stood tapping one paw, stirring up dirt. "When are you coming home?" the animal asked.

The coyote was often a trickster. It could be a warning not to be tricked by foolish appearances. The spirit of the coyote sometimes reminded a person not to take things too seriously and to find a better balance of wisdom and playfulness in one's life.

Kianso stirred in his bed, flipped to his other side, punched the pillow, and squeezed his eyes closed tighter, trying to keep the dream out. But it was useless. His feet just kept moving away from the coyote.

He passed a small stream as he moved farther along the path. He came to a rickety, wooden suspension bridge, the path continuing across it. What was on the other side, he wondered.

He glanced behind him, aware of the curious nature of the dream. But then again, it was just a dream. Nothing of importance. So he placed one foot in front of the other as he moved along the wooden boards of the bridge. The structure wobbled side to side but accepted his weight. His heart thudded in his chest. Sliding his hand along the cable that also served as a railing, he slowly progressed, fixing his gaze on the other side. The bridge swayed with every step he took. It should only take a few minutes to cross. No big deal. He wasn't afraid of heights. But the idea that the structure might give way made his pulse speed up. He had to trust that it was sturdy enough.

A distinct nervousness built inside his chest. The crossing was something bigger, something he couldn't explain. It was as if he was being drawn to something he'd been avoiding for a very long time. He breathed in the fresh aromas of the forest around him.

When he reached the other side of the bridge, he jumped off it. His feet struck solid ground. He paused, inhaling and exhaling.

See? Nothing to worry about.

The path continued, rising to a higher altitude with the terrain. At the third sharp bend in the road, a hawk landed on a low branch. "When are you coming home?" it asked.

The question was really getting irritating. What

home were they even speaking of? Hawaii? He didn't have anyone left there.

He turned away from the hawk and stayed on the path. After a slow, winding hike up a mountain, he reached a dead end. He peered out over the land below. It wasn't the highest mountain he'd explored, but the view was gorgeous.

A roar sounded off to his right, and he turned. A huge bear was lying in a field of yellow flowers, one gigantic paw resting atop the other. Bears represented grounding forces, strength, and courage. As a spirit animal in touch with the earth and the cycles of nature, it was a powerful guide to support physical and emotional healing. This animal was both feared and admired for its strength.

Kianso knew what it was going to say before it spoke.

"When are you coming home?" the bear asked.

Facing the animal, Kianso opened his heart and looked inside himself. He had shut out his shamanic ways of the past and left them back in Hawaii when he'd buried his sister. He had been living his life just fine without them. However, the journey he'd just taken had been intensely real. He had no doubt there was a message he was meant to respond to within it. But he was not going home.

A loud bang jerked him awake. He sat straight up in bed and glanced about. Another sharp clap followed. It sounded like doors closing—the first like the outer door, and the second like Seth's bedroom. The archangel was probably just getting back from his night out.

With a sigh, Kianso dropped back onto the mattress. He turned his head to check the clock on the nightstand: *3:00 a.m.*

He groaned, closed his eyes, and leaned back onto the pillow. It must be nice not to need sleep.

4

For someone who was in love with food, Seth sure
had a bare pantry. He'd said he needed to go
shopping and he wasn't kidding. At least there was
coffee and instant creamer. But that was about it
other than canned goods.

The archangel strolled into the kitchen. "I told
you we needed to go to the store."

"I'd say so," Kianso said, setting the almost-
empty jar of instant creamer on the counter.

"Don't even bother," Seth said as he turned back
to his room. "Throw some clothes on and we'll
head out."

He made a face as he took a sip of his coffee.
Yuck. No sugar.

Minutes later, he met Seth out front, both of
them fully dressed. "Normally, I just hoof it around

Nocturne Falls, but since we're going to get groceries, we'll take your car."

"No problem."

They got the car from the valet and climbed in.

"First stop," Seth said, "coffee."

"*Real* coffee," Kianso clarified.

Seth gave him directions to Black Cat Boulevard and the Hallowed Bean. They walked into the café to find that the place was hopping for a Saturday morning, especially for a town with so many night-creature residents. As expected, this hour catered to the human variety.

Kianso ordered coffee and an enormous banana muffin. Seth raved over the joint's cookies and got a dozen. "Some for now and some for later." He winked at the cashier.

She giggled, then leaned forward, whispering, "I love your wings."

"Thanks," he shot over his shoulder as he turned, heading toward a seat.

Kianso rolled his eyes. What a flirt.

A table opened up, and he snatched it. They sat and ate in the sort of silence that allowed the sleep deprived to truly wake up. The muffin tasted delicious, and the coffee rivaled the best he'd ever had back home. And that was saying a lot, because back in Hawaii, there was this little place that ground and brewed a secret blend. It was what Kianso measured all coffee against. He inhaled the aroma and downed the last of it while it was still hot.

Then he pushed back in his seat and tried to relax. His brain advised him to chill out, that he was here on vacation, but his stomach and chest wouldn't cooperate, and they cramped and tensed. His dream last night niggled at him, always within reach of his awareness, always there to intrude upon his thoughts.

Seth picked up a flyer folded in a triangle on the table. "Hey, there's a car show this weekend at the fairgrounds. Wanna go?"

Kianso shrugged. "Sure. Whatever you want to do."

As soon as Seth finished his sixth cookie, they left to make room for other customers. Kianso was about to jump into his convertible when a spirit horse revealed itself, its mane flowing in the breeze. Every muscle within him tightened. He glanced at Seth, who appeared to stand tall with respect.

"Kianso. Brah," the horse said. "Why do you avoid your nature? Why have you shut me out?"

His knees nearly buckled hearing it, and his stomach sank. The voice was that of his sister. This time, she'd come to him embodied in a horse spirit animal, one of the hardest animals to read.

He swallowed hard. "I would never shut you out," he said emphatically.

"But you have," she said. "When you left Hawaii and turned from the shamanic ways."

Instead of swinging a leg over and leaping into the driver's seat the way he had been planning to, he reached for the car door handle. When he looked back at the horse, it was gone. He tensed further, simultaneously wanting to run after her and to flee.

What was going on?

He glanced at Seth. "Did you see her?"

"Yes." The archangel nonchalantly rubbed his jaw as if contemplating something.

He wondered if this was all coincidence...with Seth showing up and talking him into a weekend trip and his sister hacking into his life. Not that he didn't want to see her, but it was unnerving. A rush of the pain he'd left behind swept through him and settled in his chest. The agony he'd run away from was there, fresh, as if he had never been free of it. All his doubts about that day and all his feelings of inadequacy bubbled up.

No, he had been right to leave Hawaii and the memories behind. He had made a new life for himself, one that didn't require his faulty shamanic customs.

He slid into the driver's seat, started the engine, and drove to the Shop 'n Save they had passed on their way into town.

Seth didn't say anything more about the spirit horse and neither did Kianso. "We only need a few staples," Seth said. "Coffee, creamer, sugar, some snacks, maybe a sandwich for lunch. For everything else we can eat out while I show you more of the town."

The archangel took the lead through the store, Kianso following along with the handheld basket. When they were finished with their selections, he paid for the items while Seth chatted with a man at the door with a cart filled to the brim.

As Kianso approached, the man extended his hand. "Hey, I'm Nick. Welcome to Nocturne Falls. Seth was just saying that this is your first time here."

"Pleased to meet you," Kianso said, shaking Nick's rock-solid hand. "Yes, I live in Tyler."

"I've heard of it," Nick said in a no-nonsense tone. Then he got straight to the point. "I'm throwing a party tonight to celebrate my friends Van and Monalisa's engagement. I told Seth you two should come."

"Oh, thanks," Kianso said, surprised. "That's very kind of you. But I don't want to intrude."

"No. No intrusion. Seth is an old friend. Please, it's at my house."

Seth looked at Kianso, who shrugged. "I'm the outsider, here," he said to the archangel. "It's up to you."

Seth looked at Nick and nodded.

"Good. Then I'll see you guys tonight." Nick turned and pushed his loaded cart into the parking lot.

"Man, the people here are nice," Kianso commented as he and Seth returned to the Mustang. He pulled out of the lot and headed back toward the condo.

"Yes. I think they're an outgoing group since they don't have to hide who they are. Nick is a gargoyle, by the way. He's in charge of security at the fountain, among other things."

"Really? There are a lot of layers to this town, aren't there? A lot of nuances the human population doesn't see?" Kianso speculated.

"Correct."

"How is it possible to keep all this secret?" Kianso waved his hand, indicating the streets of orange, black, and purple as he drove past.

"The water from the falls has special…features, let's say. It has the power to blur the edges of reality that keep humans from discovering the truth. To them, Nocturne Falls is just a marketing gimmick."

"Wow."

"But to us supernaturals, it's freedom." Seth seemed thoughtful for a moment. "Hey, after we drop the groceries at home, I should go buy a gift for tonight. You're welcome to tag along or hang at the condo. Your choice."

"No problem," Kianso said. "I'll go with."

"Excellent. Why don't you keep the motor running while I run in and put these away?"

Kianso nodded, and Seth lifted the handful of grocery bags and exited. "I'll only be a moment."

While Seth was gone, Kianso checked his e-mail and messages on his phone. Since it was the weekend, there weren't many. His Tuesday-morning meeting had been cancelled, though, and the client had left him a note to reschedule. It was an estate planning meeting, so it was nothing of dire importance or something that couldn't be handled at a later date. His client had probably gotten into his holiday weekend and decided to take an extra day or something. He couldn't blame the guy. Kianso was beginning to feel that way himself.

The car door opened, and Seth dropped back into the seat. "Geez, it's getting hot."

"Nah, it's not that bad. Compared to Hawaii, this is nothing." Kianso put the car in gear and the breeze kicked up as they moved, cooling things down. The convertible was great as long as they were moving, but when parked, it made him long for air-conditioning.

"Let's head downtown to Jack O' Lantern Lane," Seth said. "That's where Illusions is, the jewelry store that Nick's fiancée, Willa, owns. I'm sure she'll know exactly what I should get the couple."

Kianso followed Seth's instructions. They parked outside the shop and went inside.

Illusions turned out to be a lovely, quaint

specialty jewelry store. The problem was, the moment he had set foot inside, he wanted out. The place reeked of happy magic. It swirled and swelled around him, nudging at his shamanic instinct. He swallowed hard, resisting its pull. He had to keep that part of him locked away.

He fought to concentrate on Seth's conversation with Willa. The archangel had made introductions and asked Willa for gift suggestions for Van and Monalisa.

"I have the perfect gift," she said, smiling.

Her blond hair swished as she led the way to a glass curio cabinet. She opened it and took out an obelisk-shaped tower and balanced it on her opened palm. "It's called a blessings stone. This piece is made of jadeite, you can tell due to the hues of green, blue, teal, and black running through it. Jade is a gemstone that is known to encourage positive growth in life. It provides a peaceful and serene field of energy through which to achieve good luck, peace, and insight. The shape is a natural cleanser that repels negative energy from the living space."

Kianso drew nearer to the stone. "It's stunning. I can feel its link between the mortal and immortal worlds." He inhaled a long breath as its properties bathed him in the mystic presence of the energies around him. He could feel the doorways he'd so solidly slammed shut after his parents' and sister's deaths begin to crack open—doorways to other realms of reality where helping spirits resided.

"I'll take it," Seth said. "Can you gift wrap it for me?"

Willa nodded. "Of course."

"May I see the stone before you wrap it?" Kianso asked, unable to control his compulsion to touch the stone.

"Certainly. Take a look while I ring up the purchase and get the wrapping paper." She slipped the jadeite into his outstretched hand.

He sighed deeply, and warmth spread through him. Despite his denial of his gifts, he felt the coming of great change, the calling to become a seeker of light once more.

Suddenly, he stiffened. No. The light had taken his sister and parents. He gently placed the blessings stone on the counter without saying a word.

Seth and Willa looked at him with knitted brows.

"Are you all right?" Willa asked.

"Yes, thanks," Kianso answered, voice soft. His fingers trembled, and he thrust his hands into his jean pockets. "Your friends are lucky to receive such a beautiful gift."

Perhaps they would be the kind of seeker he no longer was.

5

Sasha was bored. She flew through town searching for something to entertain her. The Enchanted Garden Floral Shop proved to be an animal-friendly establishment with a darling courtyard entrance, complete with birdbath and feeder. She'd visited here for several days now. There were a couple of wrought iron benches strategically placed in the shade. She waited for the feeding hour to wrap up, and when the other birds took off, she ventured closer to the birdbath, taking a seat on the edge of the basin. A fountain spilled into the bowl, and she leaned in and drank. The water tasted clear and cool. Hopefully it was fresh and not simply circulated from the bath. Yuck.

The owner's daughter, Saffron, replenished the feeders every afternoon once the feeding frenzy had ended. Sasha waited patiently.

"You're such a sweet birdie," Saffron said. "Not pushy like the others."

"Thank you," Sasha said in her parrot voice. Of course, she wasn't like the other birds—she was a feline shifter. Perhaps that's the reason the others left whenever she arrived. Perhaps it had nothing to do with being done eating and everything to do with sensing she was different. Whatever the reason, it was fine by her.

Saffron sat on one of the benches, watching while Sasha nibbled on seed. She guessed it was instinct that drove her to eat. Caroline had also set out birdseed. The body of a bird was small compared to a human, and the kernels she consumed didn't satisfy her. Still, at the moment it wasn't so much that she was hungry as she liked the company.

"Saffron?" the little girl's mother called from inside the flower shop.

"Coming, Momma." She jumped up and looked over her shoulder. "See you later!"

Not if I can figure out a way to get rid of this horrible spell...

With a thrust of her feet and flap of her wings, she launched into the air. Flying was the one thing she liked about being a bird; she might even miss it when it was all over.

Her gaze skimmed the street, and she spotted a dreamy guy sitting in a blue Mustang in front of

Illusions. She executed a deep dive and perched on a wire not far from him. She dipped her head and then straightened abruptly. It was the same guy she'd been eyeing last night at Mummy's!

Damn, he was gorgeous. He had a deep tan and his short hair was spiked fashionably. He drummed his fingers on the side mirror as if waiting for someone to exit the store.

She flew closer, landing on the THIRTY-MINUTE PARKING sign, right in front of his car.

He stared at her, narrowing his eyes. His brow furrowed.

Sasha filled her birdy lungs with air. "What a hunk."

He leaned forward, a dreamy smile curling his lips.

Dear Gods, had she said that out loud? Her heart fluttered. And hell's bells, he gave her an odd feeling—calm and excited at the same time. She ruffled her feathers.

Gradually, he extended his palm, motioning for her to come to him.

What? Did he expect her to land on his hand?

It was an unexpected invitation…

Moving entirely on intuition, she glided and rested on his open palm, staring at him, studying him, trying to figure out why she felt this heady connection to him. For some reason, she trusted him to keep her safe, to—

The jewelry store door opened, and the angel the man had been with at Mummy's strolled toward the car. Sasha took to the air once more.

She couldn't explain it, but she saw both men as warriors in their own way—rugged, dominant protectors, embodied with strength, courage, and determination.

She headed into a tall pine and waited for her heart to stop pounding.

As the gray bird flew away, a hawk crossed her path. At least he thought she was a female. He sensed it somehow.

The hawk intruded on his thoughts. *You must own your power, be the visionary and seer and healer you were meant to be.*

Kianso clenched his jaw, aware he was being thrust in a direction he didn't want to go.

"What in the hell were you doing holding a bird?" Seth asked, climbing into the car and closing the door.

"A bird in the hand is worth two in the bush," Kianso muttered.

Seth rolled his eyes. "Ugh, I've never liked that idiom. Way too safe. It discourages taking chances."

"Whatever." Kianso wasn't sure why he'd even spouted it. Perhaps because both the hawk and

Seth had caught him off guard. He tried to shake his sullen mood as he drove.

"Hungry?" he asked the archangel.

"Oh yeah. Let's hit Howler's on the way home."

Sasha paced atop the picnic table in Caroline's backyard. She hopped effortlessly over the spaces between the wooden planks. Since this afternoon, she'd had a whole lot of free time. And no matter what she did, she kept thinking of the man in the Mustang. He had nice hands, she recalled. And she couldn't believe she trusted him, enough that she'd perched on his hand without fear or concern.

She stretched and refolded her wings. Her friend hadn't returned from work yet.

Caroline owned a small three-bedroom house on Crossbones Drive. It was a nice place with lots of trees, a fenced-in backyard, and plenty of room for pets, which she had, of course. Three dogs and three cats lounged somewhere around the house. Caroline had wanted to keep the number even, so as not to play favorites, she'd explained.

Sasha snorted. That was Caroline—always the diplomat.

The purr of the VW pulling into the driveway drifted into the backyard. Sasha flew to the roof and peered out front.

Good. Caroline was home.

Anxiety didn't begin to describe the tension simmering in Sasha's stomach. She desperately needed to connect with the witches of Nocturne Falls, and tonight was her chance.

She flew down and into the house, passing Caroline as she held open the front door.

"Hey, wait until I put my stuff down before you fly into me," Caroline said with a laugh.

Sasha landed on the back of a chair at the kitchen table. In the dining room, a tiny bird popped out of Caroline's grandfather clock and chirped five maddening times.

Nothing like being a bird listening to a fake bird to annoy the heck out you.

The wonderful thing was, on the clock's final chirp, Sasha changed into her human form. She stretched, extending her arms over her head and then bending over to touch her toes. She finished by elongating the muscles of her hips and back.

"How was your day?" Sasha asked, trying not to be as pushy as she felt. What she really wanted to do was get to Nick's place for the engagement party and talk to the witches. But she was well aware that she needed to chill and move slowly in that respect. She was essentially crashing the event, which wasn't something she was very comfortable with. It was a special occasion, and she didn't want to do anything to detract from the couple.

She inhaled a deep, calming breath. "Mind if I take a shower?" she asked.

"I told you," Caroline said, "make yourself at home."

Sasha smiled. "Thanks."

"It's my pleasure."

"What time do you want to leave?" Sasha sauntered to the fridge, opened it, and peered inside, looking for a snack to eat before she got ready. She grabbed a cheese stick. As she peeled the wrapper back, Fritz, a male dachshund, trotted over and sat up on his hind legs.

"Fritz, stop begging," Caroline admonished.

The wiener dog held his position, eyes intently fixed on Sasha. She didn't mind; she always saved the last bite of her food for the animals, anyway.

Caroline grinned. "Since Nick's place is right next door, we'll head out at six. 'Kay?"

Sasha nodded, and then tossed the wrapper in the trash. "Sounds good."

She tried to sound positive and happy, even though her anxiety was skyrocketing. The time constraints on her human form sucked. It was better than nothing, of course, but she would have only about an hour to plead her case to Pandora and the others.

With a sigh, she spun toward the spare bedroom and bath. She took a shower, blow-dried her hair, dabbed on a bit of makeup, and dressed in the black pants and coral top she'd purchased yesterday. Her favorite band of arm beads completed the outfit. She slipped on the stretchy string, settling the pale pink and ivory crystals an inch or so above her elbow. Rotating, she checked the look in the mirror, satisfied. Since the top was a bare shoulders style, she had bought a coordinating wrap for her shoulders to ward off the chill.

Caroline was in the kitchen when Sasha entered the living area. "Wow. You look great!"

"Thanks. It feels good to dress up a little." She paused as her throat caught. "It's been so long since things have been…normal."

Caroline closed the distance between them and wrapped her in a hug. "We'll figure this out and undo the spell. Don't you worry."

All Sasha could do was nod.

6

Kianso and Seth arrived slightly late to the engagement party. Evidently Seth had issues with being on time. Most of the guests had already arrived, including the guests of honor. The couple hung by the hors d'oeuvres chatting with people.

Seth presented them with his gift. "Congratulations," he said, shaking Van's hand and kissing MonalLisa, first on one cheek and then the other. The archangel could really pull out the charm when he wanted to.

"I'm honored you are in town and could attend," Van said, his Russian accent evident. "It is good to see you."

Seth dipped his head. "I feel the same."

He introduced Kianso to Van, and the two men shook hands.

"You should visit more often. Both of you," Van said. "Nocturne Falls is a nice place."

"I know. That's why I purchased a condo in town," Seth said.

Kianso's gaze shot past the two men in front of him, tuning out their banter as he eyed a woman out on the veranda. Last night, she'd fled into the streets in front of the restaurant and he'd lost her. Now, here she was.

She wore a coral halter top and black skinny jeans that hugged her slim, yet shapely bottom. There was a delicacy about her frame...as if she might break easily. A band of shimmering beads wrapped her upper arm. Slowly, she turned her head and peered at him over a bare shoulder. A jolt hit him in the chest. He was inexplicably drawn to her.

"Excuse me," he said to Seth and Van, and then began walking in her direction without taking his eyes off her. He wasn't going to lose her this time.

He watched her as she wrapped her arms about her waist, hugging herself. His first thought was something was wrong. From deep inside him, a vision sprang forth. He inhaled sharply. He'd seen her before in a dream years ago...before he'd even fled Hawaii. Suddenly he recalled that he'd felt a link with her then, and he sensed a stronger bond with her now.

A group of women formed a semicircle around her. As he approached, he picked up bits of conversation. Someone mentioned that she was under a spell that only allowed her to be in human form for a few hours each day, and she was desperate to get back to normal. Though he wasn't sure what normal was.

One thing he did know without question was that this woman was meant for him. It was more than love at first sight. It was two souls being connected. He understood how it was possible. At least from a shamanic point of view. But he also realized the feelings were not necessarily mutual or even that a union was a sure thing. There was many a man who missed his soul mate due to misconceptions.

Kianso tensed, unsure what her reaction to him would be. Even so, he strolled right up to her and extended his hand in greeting. "Hello. I'm Kianso Oka Kane. I couldn't help overhearing that you have a bit of a problem."

She froze, gazing into his eyes. Her long, dark lashes dipped slowly down and then back up as she took his hand. Electricity shot through him at her touch.

"I-I'm Sasha," she said.

"Is there something I can do to help?" he asked.

The striking young blonde stepped forward, separating herself from the group slightly. "That's very kind of you to come to my aid. Honestly, I can use all the help I can get with this stupid spell, but I'm not sure there's anything you can do."

Her words somehow warmed him from the inside out. He examined the assembly of women again. He opened up his senses in a way he hadn't since he'd left Hawaii.

"I doubt there's anything you can do," the woman closest to him said with a slight laugh. She had a brunette bobbed hairdo, whiskey-brown eyes, and a petite build. "Not unless you're a warlock or sorcerer." She held out her hand for him to shake. "I'm Charisma, the middle sister."

"Witches? You're all witches?" he asked in an even tone.

"Bingo. Give the man a prize," Marigold said.

"I'm not." Caroline raised her hand, singling herself out. He got the feeling that she wanted him to know there was at least one approachable person among them.

"Ladies, meet the witch doctor," Pandora said, raising a manicured brow.

"Shaman," he corrected with a smile.

She smiled congenially back. "Sorry. When we all get together we get a little out of hand. May I introduce the witches of Nocturne Falls?" She quickly pointed out each female witch in the group as she went around the circle. "My sisters, Charisma and Marigold; my mother, Corette; Dominique; Martha; and our high priestess, Alice."

"Ladies." He nodded. "It's a pleasure to meet you." Absently, he realized he'd never been in the company of so much power in all his life.

Caroline lightly touched Sasha's arm. "We need to hurry and get things set up."

Sasha eased forward again, her eyes pleading to him. "Please allow us some privacy. I don't have much time."

He held out his hand, hoping she'd place hers in his. "I might be able to help."

Accepting his offered hand, she eased into his personal space. He wrapped her hand in both of his.

"Unfortunately, I don't know if *anyone* can help." She scanned the area nervously. "And I don't want to detract from the festivities. I only came here to introduce myself to the coven and learn if there is anything they could do. I'll be leaving in"—she glanced at her watch and shifted closer to the women—"a few minutes."

Pandora placed a hand on her hip, standing tall and regal. "Don't worry. The coven will take your case under advisement."

He wondered if she was the oldest sister. She seemed to take charge.

Sasha smiled weakly. "Good. I can't tell you how much I appreciate it. I just don't know what else to do."

Her distress tugged at his heart. He wanted to draw her into an embrace and hold her.

"Explain to us what happened," Pandora added.

Her throat worked before Sasha spoke. "I had a

misunderstanding with my friend, Lilly Reese. She got the wrong impression from her boyfriend that we had gotten together or something. In her anger, she cast a hex on me. And now—" she spread her arms wide, palms up "—I'm only human for three hours out of the day."

"Geez. You do need our help," Charisma said.

"The alternative is to live out the duration of the spell," another witch commented.

"I don't even know how long that will be," Sasha said sadly. Then suddenly, with no fanfare at all, she shifted into a bird.

Kianso sucked air into his lungs. If he wasn't mistaken, she was the same bird he'd encountered downtown that afternoon.

The group of witches gasped in unison.

"Poor girl," one of them whispered.

Kianso held out the back of his hand. The bird perched on it. "Don't worry," he said. "We'll figure this out together."

He was standing in the middle of the veranda among the group of witches when Seth marched up, seeming distressed.

Seth leaned in, saying under his breath, "I'm sorry, Five-O, but I have to bug out. I received a summons from the Divine Tree in Japan." He dropped keys into Kianso's free hand. "I feel bad deserting you, but make yourself at home for as long as you like." Seth knuckled-bumped his shoulder.

Kianso was taken aback. He was still reeling over what was happening with Sasha. Surprised by the turn of events, he nodded, regaining his composure. "Okay, man. No problem."

With that, Seth saluted the ladies. He hustled into the backyard and flew upward until he vanished into a speck of bright light.

Behind him, he heard one of the witches whisper to another. "I like that archangel. I really do."

The bird climbed up his arm onto his shoulder. He glanced around, his eyes at last settling on Pandora, drawing on his lawyer persona. "I'll be staying at Seth's condo at the Excelsior for the next few days. If you should come up with a strategy for Sasha, please contact me. I'd really be grateful."

"I have a place there, also," Charisma said, "So we can easily stay in touch."

For a few seconds, he stood there meeting the gazes of the witches. They were all beautiful women, and by the nods of their heads and sympathetic expressions, they seemed willing to come to Sasha's aide.

"Pandora, you may consult my library and see if there is remedy to the spell," Corette said, nodding. "If necessary, we will contact the ACW for suggestions."

He had no clue what she was talking about. He squinted at her and his brow furrowed.

"The American Council of Witches," she said by

way of explanation. "There are rules about casting a spell in anger," Corette added. "Rest assured. We're here to help."

Kianso glanced around, past the small gathering on the porch. He wanted to start figuring this out now, this minute. "So, when do we leave? If there's any way I can help, just say the word."

Pandora strolled by him and paused to pat his cheek. "Patience. I don't want to interfere with the festivities. We'll begin tomorrow."

Everyone seemed to agree. This wasn't the time nor the place to pursue the problem at hand. The group dispersed, returning to the celebration. Kianso hung around for an hour or so, and while everyone was very friendly and inviting, he still felt like an outsider. Seth had been the one truly invited to this shindig, and he was gone.

Caroline kindly filled in the gap, introducing him around. But even though she made the extra effort, he could tell she didn't move among the inner circles of the town. Not like Seth did. Finally, shortly after nine o'clock, he said goodnight and headed out.

Sasha had stayed perched on his shoulder the entire time he remained at the party, but outside on the front porch, she flew from him to Caroline. "I live next door if you need anything," she explained. "You can find me there or at the pet shop."

"Okay," he said, smiling his thanks. "I'll check in tomorrow."

7

The room's ambient lighting radiated a peaceful glow, yet the silence made him well aware he was alone in Seth's condo.

Kianso flipped the switch on the wall that controlled the automatic window shades and rolled them up. He had learned this evening that Julian Ellingham owned the penthouse suite. The builders had considered everyone's comfort in the design of the condos, hence the tinted windows. It was a nice touch. He could get used to this place.

He stood at the window gazing out into the night. The moon hung low in the cloudless western sky, a fat crescent of the last quarter bright and clear. Jupiter shone near it. Spiritual energy swirled around him, filling every crevice and pressing against him, suffocating him. The shaman connection was automatic and something he had to struggle to ignore. He tensed and fisted his hands.

He'd opened the door tonight to that mystical pathway. Darn it, for eight years he'd managed to keep it locked shut. Now, because of his feeling for Sasha, he'd ventured onto the path of healer again. He worried if the love he felt was true, or a false reading...like he'd had with his family.

Turning from the window, Kianso kicked back in the plush leather recliner and finally closed his eyes. He'd stayed up all night, projecting a panther protection on Sasha. Through the spirit animal, he'd guarded her in her sleep. And while he was miserable on one level because he'd given in to his shamanic calling, the part of him joined to Sasha felt damn fine. He liked watching over her.

But seeing her in bird form wasn't nearly as engaging as when she was in her human form. Still, he could feel in his bones that it was his duty now to watch over her. The witch who had cast the spell on her had done so maliciously, and his law experience told him that vicious people rarely stopped with a single act of violence. Sometimes they carried a huge grudge forever, letting out their anger on others here and there for as long as they lived.

That thought prompted others: What if the witches couldn't solve her problem? Was it possible they couldn't reverse the spell? That she would have to live in this limbo forever? That he would only get to be with her three hours of every day?

TU Kai, he swore, reverting to a Hawaiian expletive.

He got up and walked over to Seth's well-stocked bar and poured himself a glass of bourbon. He took a nervous sip, then shook his head resolutely.

No. The witches would find a remedy. They had to.

He took another drink, trying not to worry about Sasha. Like every other case he'd ever represented, this wasn't something he would give up on. She would be free once more.

Usually the nights passed quickly for Sasha. She'd sleep through the night when nothing bothered her, and it didn't matter if she was cat or bird or human. Her dreams were all similar in nature, showing her a time when she was free of the curse.

But tonight, an odd manifestation of dreams kept the peace at bay. She tossed restlessly. Her thoughts turned repeatedly to the shaman and his thoughtfulness in wanting to help her. When he'd introduced himself, his lingering handshake and easy manner had melted her tension away instantly. No stuffy pretense with this guy. His shoulders and chest were broad, as if he'd been swimming his entire life, and even though he had a tall, muscular frame, he moved with a laid-back grace.

She recalled his kind, golden eyes and handsome smile. A hint of a dimple nudged one of his cheeks. She had longed to place her palm there and ease his face closer to hers.

She jerked awake, and the feeling that she was being watched by someone washed over her. She glanced around, her instincts on high alert. Someone was in the room.

She shifted in the nest she'd created from a soft scarf. The silk rubbed against her feathers as she strained, leaning forward to see across the room better. There, on the other side of the space, a large black panther lounged in the bright moonlight. His yellow-green eyes angled up to stare at her.

Her breath caught, and for a moment, she wondered if she was still dreaming. She rose and stretched, and then flew across the room to a large, sturdy vase on a table. The cat tracked her movements with its eyes but didn't budge. She dropped down and hopped cautiously across the floor, closer to the panther, and stopped a foot or so from its big paws. Her senses were going haywire because what she saw and what she felt conflicted. On one hand, the animal didn't seem real. On the other, her brain warned her to be careful. And then, the strangest thing happened: the cat faded away like a hot breath on a cold day.

Sasha's heart raced, uncertainty getting the best of her, as she moved over to the spot where the panther had been seconds earlier. Nothing. It had completely vanished.

Maybe it had been part of her dream state? *A real panther can't just disappear like that.* She couldn't help the hard laugh that bubbled out of her at the irony—*she* could disappear like that now, shifting from human to bird in the blink of an eye. She sighed. This was crazy. But whatever the panther was, it felt like a friend watching over her. Perhaps her lack of fear could be attributed to her own cat-shifting nature—like recognizing like.

She trotted back to her nest and snuggled into the scarf once more, returning to her thoughts of Kianso. Some unknown force kept calling her to him, telling her that was where she belonged.

After some time of restlessness, she flew to the window and looked out. The sky was already brightening with the rising sun. Caroline would be up and getting ready to head to the shop. Today was Sunday, so the store wouldn't be open, but she still had to tend to the animals. There was no day off for that.

Besides, it gave Sasha the opportunity to seek out Kianso. Because if she had to endure this dreadful form, at least she could pursue the connection she felt with him.

She winged through the house to find Caroline.

She was at the kitchen sink, filling the coffee pot with water. "Morning," Sasha said.

"Hey there," Caroline replied.

"I thought I'd let you know, I'm hanging with Kianso today."

Caroline glanced over her shoulder. "You like him, don't you?"

"Yes. I like him a lot."

The layout of the condo underscored its functionality. The bedrooms were located on the northwest side of the building, and the kitchen and nook were on the east, which meant he could watch the sun rise over the tree line while drinking his coffee. The scene was picturesque in its own way, but it was a far cry from his home in Hawaii where the sun sprang up from the ocean. He missed that. He missed a lot of things.

While he sipped his coffee, the day grew brighter. The sun glistened through the trees, catching the morning dew. A bird settled on the top of the flagpole in front of the building. With its unmistakable green color, he felt certain it was Sasha. She turned her head left and right, seeming to be looking for something.

Could she have come to him? He set his mug aside. There was one way to find out. He exited through the front door.

Downstairs, the valet eyed him as he walked out onto the drive in his robe. "Is there anything I can do for you, sir?" the man asked.

"No. I thought I saw something of interest out the window...a bird." Kianso glanced toward the top of the flagpole, but the bird was gone. He perused the rest of the area.

"There are many birds around here," the valet said.

"This one is of particular interest to me."

As he shuffled back toward the entrance, a chirp made him turn his head. The green Quaker parrot had perched on the bench. She chirped again.

"Hey, there." He held out his arm for her to come to him. She immediately winged over and landed on the back of his extended hand.

"Oh good. You found it," the valet said.

"Yes." He brushed the crook of his index finger over her head and down the back of her neck. She leaned into his touch. He proceeded through the entry doors, heading back to the suite.

When they were back inside the condo, he went to the kitchen and fixed himself another cup of coffee. "Are you thirsty? Do you want something to drink?"

"Water, please," she said in her shrill bird voice.

He set a cup of water on the table, and she moved over to it. Then he sliced a sweet roll down the middle and placed one half on a napkin before her.

"Thank you."

He sat and ate his half of the sweet roll while she pecked at hers. "Finished?" he asked when she seemed to have had enough.

"Yes."

He cleared the table and cleaned up. Then he kicked back in the leather recliner with his laptop. She flew over and perched on his shoulder. "I'm doing some research on spells," he told her.

"I've done some."

He tried to interpret the key words she'd spoken. He'd noticed that at times she conserved her speech. "You've done some research already?"

She bobbed her head.

He paused, tightening his jaw.

Let go of the old and renew yourself, his sister's voice whispered to him. He glanced around, trying to find her. But she didn't seem to take a form.

Did you hear me?

He balled his fist over the keyboard, frustrated. He didn't want to keep reverting to shamanism as he had with the panther the night before.

But Sasha needed answers, and the spirit guides could have solutions. He sighed. "I'm going to ask my spirit animals. Perhaps they know of a way to rid you of this spell."

It couldn't hurt to check, he guessed. He closed his eyes and called on them to share new forms of guidance.

As he mentally prepared himself to enter a trance, he spoke to Sasha. "I'm going to access my dream state—" He paused, wondering what she'd think of this. "Don't be alarmed if I'm unresponsive for a bit. My kind have been doing this since the beginning of time. Evidence can be found in rock art and cave art since the Ice Age."

Listen to the spirits of your ancestors, his sister said. *Heed the advice of the angelic forces.*

Even though that's exactly what he was contemplating, he fought against Jen's advice. "I haven't called upon my guides in a long time. I gave it up after my parents' and sister's deaths," he admitted, the pain of their loss still searing his insides.

The Quaker nuzzled his cheek. "I'm sorry."

They both jumped as a hawk materialized on the coffee table in front of them. "Life doesn't always go the way you expect it. You have to accept change. Accept the life you are guided to live," the hawk said in his sister's feminine voice.

Sasha trotted along his arm to his hand, seeming to be intently looking at the hawk, as though she also could see it.

So what do you want to do? his sister asked him pointedly, her hawk wings braced tightly to her sides.

8

The hawk mesmerized her. Its presence was quite similar to that of the panther last night—with it kind of mysteriously *there*, and yet not solid or palpable. She didn't know exactly what shamans did, but there seemed to be a connection between the animals and Kianso.

"I want to free Sasha from the curse placed on her," Kianso said, his voice rumbling strong and authoritative.

He spoke like a man used to being in control, she thought. A man who didn't accept no for an answer. A man—or lawyer—who loved to win. But at the same time, he seemed gentle and caring.

She fluttered her wings. "Thank you."

She glanced at the clock, even though she internally knew the time. Six hours, twenty-three

143

minutes, and eleven seconds before she transformed into her human self again. It felt like a lifetime before she'd be able to talk to him—*really* talk to him in more than these monosyllabic responses. Plus, she simply wanted to know more about this striking, complex man.

She turned and traveled back up his arm to his shoulder. Right there was where she would stay until she could change into her real self.

He set his jaw as he tapped the keys on his computer, flipping from one e-mail correspondence to the other. He had posted her problem to a group of his psychic friends. While she was interested in what he was learning that could help her, she tried not to read over his shoulder. The conversations were too complicated for her to comprehend, anyway, as they were speaking of entering different realms of reality, with open space and time constructs.

At one point she noticed that he was researching Quaker parrots, their behaviors, and what they ate. That was very sweet of him, she thought. He saw her looking at him and explained, "I wanted to see what to feed you so I know what to pick up."

"Thank you."

Around midafternoon, he set the computer aside and simply sat, staring straight ahead, as if focused on something far away.

Sasha angled her head one way and then the

other, wondering what he was doing. He seemed to be in a trance of some kind.

The hawk, who had remained quietly sitting on the coffee table all day, spoke up. "We call it dreaming while awake. He has moved beyond the inner doorway."

Sasha looked at the hawk in surprise. She opened and closed her beak, not quite knowing what to say.

Since the hawk appeared to be spirit instead of flesh, she didn't seem to have the same communication problem that Sasha had. "The seeker has access to a transcendent connection to the sacred realms of the spirit world. The fabric of reality is composed of a multilevel vibrational field that is conscious and intelligent. He is searching for favorable conditions in which the field will respond," the hawk explained.

"Unusual abilities," Sasha chirped, watching Kianso as he looked beyond what she could see.

"Yes. He is a talented shaman. It has pained me to see him turn from his shamanic calling since our accident."

Sasha's breath caught. Was Kianso's mother the spirit inside the hawk? She wondered who the female was.

"He has the great gifts of wisdom, power, and healing," she went on. "Our reconnection with Nature is the gateway into the invisible worlds all around us."

"Are you his mother?" Sasha asked, wanting confirmation.

The hawk shook its head. "No. I'm his sister, Jen."

Sasha's beak dropped open. She really shouldn't be surprised at what was possible anymore, but it still always awed her.

A knock sounded at the door, and Kianso's body jerked. He shifted and straightened, groaning softly as he came out of the trance.

The hawk vanished.

"It's the witches," he said, standing.

She wondered how he knew that, but she supposed it had to do with the spirits and various planes of reality. Or something.

He walked to the door and opened it wide, revealing Pandora and Charisma.

"Good afternoon," Charisma said. The greeting lacked enthusiasm.

Neither witch smiled; they just nodded and entered as Kianso invited them inside. Sasha's stomach knotted with uneasy anticipation.

"Would you like a cup of tea or a soda?" Kianso offered.

"No. Thank you," Pandora said. "We thought we should come in person to tell you what we've found."

Sasha prepared herself. By the drawn looks on their faces, it couldn't be good news.

"I appreciate that," Kianso said.

"As do I," Sasha chimed in. Pandora gave her a sympathetic smile.

Charisma wet her lips. "The spell can be broken," she started, "but only on Samhain's full moon. And only by her true love."

Sasha's heart sank. She hadn't even been on a date in over six months, never mind discovering her true love.

"Fortunately, we will have a full moon this Halloween," Pandora added.

Kianso's lips tugged upward.

Anger roiled in her chest. What did he have to smile about? Halloween was a mere three weeks away. It was impossible.

He set his left hand on his shoulder, indicating for her to step onto it. She did, and he moved her in front of him so they were eye level and between Pandora and Charisma.

"Then there is hope of freeing her of the spell," he said. "I have seen it in my visions and know it in my heart… *I* am her true love."

No sooner had he said it than she changed into her human form.

She inhaled a deep breath. "Say what?"

He put his hands in his pockets. "Don't worry. I have a few weeks to convince you, but we are destined for each other."

"Well," Pandora said, "it's simply a matter of

timing, then. We'll leave you to get to know each other." The sisters turned in unison, heading for the door.

Charisma paused outside in the hall and looked back at them. "Oh, and just a reminder. It has to be the real thing or the spell won't be broken. No love potions or getting Willa to make a special ring or anything like that."

"Charisma, hush," Pandora chastised her.

"Just telling the truth," the other witch responded.

Sasha moved closer to Kianso, threading her arm through his. She'd been perfectly content sitting on his shoulder all day. Why should she feel differently now? "Thank you for stopping by and sharing what you learned," she said with a nervous smile. "And thank you for even helping at all."

The witches nodded.

"Well, see you two around," Pandora said, waving as they left.

As soon as the door closed, he pulled Sasha into a hug. She felt so good in his arms, so right. He slid his palm up and down her back, trying to soothe her, to reassure her. "It will be okay," he said.

She dipped her head and leaned it against his shoulder. "I want to believe that."

After a moment, she stepped back and searched

his eyes. "When did you see us together? Just a while ago when you were in that trance?"

"No. It was when I was younger," he said. "When I saw you at Mummy's the other night, you seemed familiar. Like I should recognize you. But it wasn't until we were at Nick's place that it registered."

"Wow," she breathed.

He ran a gentle hand over her arm. He couldn't get enough of touching her. "Do you want to go out for a bite to eat?"

"How about we order in?" she suggested. "I'm on a schedule, you know." She let out a small giggle.

"Okay." He closed the distance between them and cupped her face in his hands as his lips claimed hers. Good heavens, she tasted wonderful. "Then I better take advantage while I can," he said against her mouth. When she broke the kiss, he let her go.

She drew in a deep tremulous breath, searching his eyes. Her hand came up and rested on his chest before she threaded her fingers in his hair and pulled him toward her, initiating a longer, more passionate kiss.

When she moaned, he pulled her tighter against his body. What a powerful aphrodisiac to know she was as attracted to him as he was to her. He wished he could touch her and kiss her all night long.

Images flashed in his head of taking her into his

bedroom. Reluctantly, he ended the kiss. As he eased to her side he said, "Um, dinner?" He tilted his head and gave her a wink. "Although I'll admit I'm hungry for far more than food.

He slid one hand into hers while pulling his phone from his pocket with the other. "Is Guillermo's all right with you? Seth told me the dishes there were excellent."

She nodded. "Sure."

They looked at the online menu and made their selections. When he called and placed their delivery order, the guy on the other end was exuberant and helpful. Kianso wondered if the Excelsior address had anything to do with the speedy response, or if they were just as nice to everyone.

He guided her to the couch and they sat down, still holding hands. He lifted hers to his lips, kissing the backs of her fingers. "I'm your soul mate," he whispered. "And I'm going to do everything in my power to prove that to you."

"I guess we'll know for sure on Halloween," she said. "If the spell is broken."

"*When* the spell is broken," he corrected, and then kissed her deeply. But even as he tasted her delicious lips, he knew the structure of destiny may have a flaw. She had to truly love him for it to work. And love reciprocated was never a given.

9

Sasha tried to shut out the tiny voice of doubt as she searched his sincere gaze. He seemed so certain. And yet she didn't really know him at all. Yes, he made her feel butterflies in her stomach when he looked at her. Yes, she definitely warmed and melted with his kiss, as her limbs turned soft as caramel. Yes, when she closed her eyes and caught his spicy masculine scent, she longed to have him stay longer.

But forever? Would what she felt last that long? She couldn't say.

For now though, she was extremely attracted to him. She *wanted* him to be the one…for a number of reasons. Perhaps most of all, she was tired of being alone. Her kind was meant to have partners…a mate for life.

Outside the window, it began to rain. She strolled closer to look out. Raindrops splattered and ran down the glass. "I love the rain. It makes everything seem clean and fresh."

He came up behind her and wrapped his arms around her waist. "So do I. It rains about seventy inches a year in Hawaii. Which means it rains somewhere on the islands nearly every day."

She laughed. "So you always know your facts?"

"I'm a lawyer. It comes naturally." He leaned in, brushing his lips against her temple. "You have a lovely laugh."

"Thank you." She watched the stream of raindrops fall. "I haven't had much to laugh about lately. It feels good."

For several long moments they stood there, looking out the window. Calm came over her—a sense that things would be all right…that the path of healing before her was as it should be. It was nice, she thought, sharing this peaceful interval, allowing her body to feel Kianso's heartbeat against her back. For months, she'd been so caught up in her own troubles, she'd thought of little else except breaking free. Every day she had spent trapped in bird form, her faith crumbled a bit more. Could he truly be the answer to her problems? She hoped so. Especially since she liked him…a lot.

"Dinner is here," he said, angling his chin toward the parking lot below.

She followed his gaze to the car sporting the restaurant name as it pulled in the drive. "Good. I'm hungry." She was also hungry for him…and everything he represented, companion, friend, lover.

The downstairs attendant rang up that dinner was here. "Excellent. Send him to the suite," Kianso said.

A few minutes later they had everything arranged on the dining table, including an exquisite bottle of wine. She inhaled an appreciative breath. "It smells divine."

"I've never eaten at Guillermo's, but Seth seemed to like it."

"I haven't been there either. I was under the impression the place was better suited for a romantic evening." She shrugged. "In my current situation, well, let's just say romance hasn't been on my list."

"It is now."

She lowered her lashes, then peeked at him again.

He gave her a look that sent a tingle all the way down to her toes. Plus, a flare of heat went straight to her tummy. "Mm, sounds good to me." And it did. She wanted to be romanced by this guy. This shaman. This spirit guide warrior who seemed to know things she didn't.

She watched his strong hands as he poured her wine and gave it to her. If she'd had to guess, she never would have placed him in a desk job. His physique suggested physical activity. Maybe he did a lot of exercise or played sports on the side. She slipped into the chair across from him.

"Smells yummy," she said.

"It sure does."

"Do you cook?" she asked.

"Only enough to get buy. But I'm the king of grilling out."

"When I lived in Montgomery, Alabama, before the curse, I used to cook a lot. In my free time, I'd take in the Cooking Channel and loved to try new recipes." She fought against the sadness of losing her life.

"Guess that doesn't work now," he said.

"Well, I can still watch the shows… I'm just in my bird form." She laughed halfheartedly, deciding to look on the bright side.

"True. Do you have any family to help you out?"

She shook her head, reaching for a piece of bread. "No. I'm an only child and my parents live in Australia. I didn't want to bother them over a lover's quarrel."

"Lover's quarrel?" His spine straightened and he stared at her with narrowed, questioning eyes.

"Perhaps that's not the right term. It wasn't my lover, but a friend's. She got angry over a misunderstanding. It wasn't my fault her guy hit on me. But she got angry anyway, and wham, bam, now I'm up close and personal with feathers."

"She doesn't sound like much of a friend."

"She wasn't. An acquaintance from work, mainly. But I learned it's best to stay on the good side of any witches."

"I'm sorry."

"Thanks." She observed him as he ate another bite of his lasagna, then rotated his fork upside down and drew it through his mouth again. The man had exquisite lips. The slightest bit full and expressive. Holy cats, she enjoyed watching the merest play of emotions roll over them. The sideways tug as he half smiled. The slight purse. The inward draw as he contemplated something she said.

Wondering how much time she had left, she glanced at her watch. Minutes. Darn it all.

He noticed her checking, but said nothing. He simply lifted her dessert fork, cut a chunk of tiramisu, and positioned it in front of her mouth. "Better finish eating."

She opened her mouth and he fed her. The dessert melted on her tongue, sweet and smooth with rich chocolate, coffee, and hint of rum flavors. The bite was too large, so she took what she could and left the rest, which promptly vanished between his lips. Warmth settled low inside her. Her tongue swept the edges of her mouth as she fought the desire to lean across the table to kiss him.

One minute she gazed into his gorgeous dark

eyes, the next all she saw was the underside of the table and found herself staring at his pants-clad thighs and crotch. Oh my.

He stood, navigating around the table to view her, extending his hand for her to step upon. "It's still early. Let's go sit in the living room."

His interaction amazed her. He could have simply viewed her as a bird, an animal of little significance. However, the warm, compassionate look in his eyes said differently. She flew to his offered hand, resting on his knuckles.

In the living room, he dropped into a recliner and flipped on the TV, bringing up the directory and stopping on the Cooking Channel. He stroked a finger over her head and down the feathers on her back. "I know we just ate and this may not be very appealing to you at the moment. Would you like me to put on something else?"

"No," she chirped. It was the sweetest thing he could have done. She scampered to his shoulder and nudged her head against his cheek. "Thank you."

The program featured a connoisseur traveling across the country sampling food. He was in Maine in this episode. "When you're back to normal, we'll have to travel to some of these restaurants mentioned on this show. I may not be the best cook, but I love to eat."

"Me too." It pleased her that they had something in common.

For a long while, they relaxed and learned about a culinary find for scrumptious seafood on the coast of Maine. Despite the show's intriguing subject, Sasha grew less interested in the program as she tuned into the man at her side.

She paid attention to his breathing and the rise and fall of his muscular pecs. She observed the pulsing vein at his throat. And she wished she were in human form so she could feel the warmth of that spot beneath her lips.

What an awful time to fall for a guy. He'd claimed to be her true mate, but she wasn't convinced. Didn't bells and whistles go off in those cases? Oh, what a mess her life was.

Kianso relaxed, allowing the last twenty-four hours to sink in. He'd reluctantly come to Nocturne Falls with Seth, simply for a getaway. Now, he'd met his mate. He didn't know whether to jump for joy or run for the hills.

A wife hadn't been anywhere on his radar.

The voice in his head taunted. *Who said she will have you?*

It was true. There was no certainty. She could deny what was destined for them. Or perhaps she could accept him only to get out of her current predicament. The last thought bothered him.

Pandora had indicated that the love between then had to be the real deal. Did that mean if she didn't truly love him, she wouldn't change? Like, if she only accepted him to get out of the curse, it wouldn't work? He suppressed a sigh. Actually, that would be a good thing, he guessed.

He wanted her love to be genuine, not forced because she was desperate to change her situation. The love element may be moving too fast for her. Even if they were meant to be together, would she feel that for him in just three weeks?

A full moon on Halloween may not come again for years.

Tightness crept into his chest. If she didn't love him now, they would be living in this limbo for a very long time.

She seemed to sense the anxiety within him. Her light steps tickled as she trekked over his chest to the hollow of his sternum. There, she settled, folding herself into a feathery ball.

He closed his eyes, getting control of his doubts.

Three weeks. He had three weeks to make her fall in love with him. His lips eased to the side…his eyes were closed. He mentally snickered. He could do that, couldn't he?

The next thing he knew the sun peeked through the windows. Cracking one eyelid open and then the other, he stole a look. Yep, it was morning.

He'd slept the entire night in the recliner with Sasha on his chest.

She twittered as he stretched. "Good morning," he said.

"Morning," she replied and then flitted around the room, landing on the back of a chair.

Since he wasn't quite sure what needs she had as a bird, he strolled to the window and cracked it open. "There. If you need to fly outside you can."

But instead she landed on his shoulder again.

"Or not."

She chirped a happy sound.

He walked into the bedroom suite. "To most people, talking to a bird may seem odd. But I speak to spirit animals all the time." He paused, remembering. "At least I *did* until I gave up that life."

With a rustle of wings, she glided to the middle of his bed. He had a moment of imagining her there in human form. It was a delicious thought of her dressed in a silky, red nightie that he would enjoy peeling off of her.

"I'm going to grab a shower," he said with the slightest catch in his voice. "Then we can eat and tour some of Nocturne Falls. Seth had mentioned a car show today. That may be fun." But was anything enjoyable for her when she was in this altered form? He'd have to ask her this evening.

10

Sasha sat on the bed feeling a bit sorry for herself. Here she was with the hottest guy she'd been with in her life, and she was stuck in the body of a bird. She inhaled and tried to put a positive spin on things.

The shower came on in the bathroom. The patter of the water beating against glass filtered through the half-open door, along with a swirl of damp air. It would have been wonderful to join him. She envisioned running her hands over his slick, hard chest and soaping him up.

Huh. What would it be like to have a real relationship with him? She realized she was toying with the possibility. Which was totally crazy given her situation. But if she were herself again? No, she barely knew the man. Still, there was something about him that touched her. Maybe it was the way he cared for her while she was a bird. Maybe if they had a real date she'd know for certain.

The bathroom door pushed fully open and Kianso strolled out with a towel wrapped around his hips. "Sorry. I forgot my clothes."

As he entered the walk-in closet, Sasha clutched the bedspread with her talons to remain in place. Oooh, she wanted to trail behind him and get another glimpse of those hard planes and perhaps even a peek at his backside when that towel slipped away. That very human part of her didn't see any harm in wishing.

She gave a long tremulous sigh.

How could he want anything to do with her?

Disappointment sliced through her as he exited the closet fully dressed, handsome as ever, wearing a button-up gray shirt and navy slacks. He carried a pair of dark brown suede penny loafers. The mattress dipped as he sat and slipped on the shoes. She stepped closer, getting a whiff of his freshly showered scent. He smelled good.

She hoped she'd be able to grab a shower this evening.

"Ready?" He paused, looking over his shoulder at her. "Can I get you anything before we go?"

"No. I'm fine."

He held out a hand for her to step upon. She did, and he placed her on his shoulder. "I'm starting to like having you with me." His voice was a gentle rumble.

He smelled even better up close. Masculine. Kissable. She rubbed the top of her head along his jaw.

Her days had gotten remarkably better with him near.

It was mid-morning by the time they arrived at the fairgrounds. The temperature gave a hint of fall. Kianso stopped by the farmer's market near the gate. He purchased some grapes that he thought Sasha might enjoy and a soda for himself.

The turnout was pretty decent. He had to wait in line to get his ticket. Evidently, the proceeds went to a worthy cause: Bridge, crisis counseling for misguidedteens of dual species. He guessed identity issues could get super confusing. What if you were part vampire and part werewolf? Or a mixture of fae and gargoyle?

Or shaman and shifter?

That's what their children would be if he and Sasha had kids. The muscles along his back tensed. It was a sobering thought. But his feelings took him to a place where he easily envisioned a life with her as his wife.

If she'd have him. He turned his head and peeked

down at his shoulder where she sat. Even if they had to live together in this limbo state she was in, she was worth it. She had the kind of spunk he admired. Here she was, making the best of a bad situation and trying to take control of finding a solution. She was something else. Beautiful, and kind, and in need of protection whether she liked it or not.

He was willing to work through their difficulties and plan a future together. He imagined the things couples did, their goals of marriage and vacations and sharing life and a family.

He looked forward to being a father, he realized. And until now, he hadn't given much thought to that. He nodded at the people he passed. Nocturne Falls would make a great place to raise a family. Yes, someday it would be nice having children with Sasha. That was one hell of a thought.

But he sensed a real relationship wouldn't happen until she was her real self again. Not because he had a problem with her unstable state of being, but because he didn't think she would allow it.

He set his jaw, determined to convince her otherwise. Yes, Nocturne Falls would make a fine hometown.

As he moved between the rows of pristine classic automobiles, he began thinking of the people as neighbors rather than strangers.

"How's it going?" Nick said as he approached Kianso at the 1954 Jaguar coupe display.

Kianso looked up. "Oh, hi. We're doing great. This is a fantastic show."

"Yes. It is," Nick said. He took in Sasha perched on his shoulder. "Pandora told me about your dilemma, Sasha. I'm so sorry."

"Thank you. But the end may be in sight," Sasha intoned, her parrot voice happy with anticipation.

"Glad to hear it." His phone vibrated in his pocket. He pulled it free and glanced down. "Willa. She wants me at the baked goods table." He nudged the phone at Kianso. "Good luck. See you later."

Nick zigzagged through the people milling around the cars. Kianso continued on to a red 1964 Corvette convertible several yards away. Sasha whistled. "Now that's my kind of wheels," she said. She flew from his shoulder and landed on the steering wheel, peering out the windshield.

He imagined her in human form, sitting in the driver's seat. The car was sexy, but she would outshine it by a mile. She would look fantastic with her white-blond hair whipping in the wind. And he liked the picture of him sitting next to her and leaning over the gearshift to steal a kiss.

"You have a dreamy look on your face," she said. "What are you thinking?"

"Of how beautiful you'd look driving this Vette."

"Too bad you don't know the owner. Maybe he'd let us take it for a spin."

It was a crazy thing to say. No stranger loans out his antique Vette. Then again, when you're under a witch's spell, isn't everything a little crazy? "Yeah. That would be fun." He played along. Actually, he would consent to any fantasy that would make her happy.

She flapped her wings and rose into the air. For a heartbeat, he felt like she was leaving him. A sinking sensation sat heavy in his stomach. Then, she banked and came back, taking her usual place on his shoulder. He couldn't help it, his lips widened into a grin.

"Don't leave me like that," he told her.

She laughed. The first he'd heard from her. The sound warmed his heart and caused his throat to tighten.

"You said we were soul mates, right? You're not going to get rid of me that easy."

The food tables formed a horseshoe at the end of the row of cars, successfully trapping the spectators. "Mmm, funnel cakes. Want to share one?"

"Sure."

He ordered and paid for the funnel cake and then found a large, shady oak away from the crowd where he parked his ass with his back pressed against the tree trunk. Sasha rested on his lap as he fed her pieces of grapes and funnel cake. No one seemed concerned about a man and his bird.

Then his cell phone rang.

11

"It was Pandora. She's been looking for us. She wants to meet," Kianso said.

"Did she say why?"

"No. But she'll meet us here. She already went by the condo. And she's on her way."

Sasha latched on to his finger with her talons and squeezed. "I hope nothing has changed. You know...that Halloween isn't the day, or something." A tightness spread throughout her chest as uncertainty leaked through the cracks in her optimism. No. There was no use getting upset yet.

Still she held firmly in place. His strong presence gave her hope.

He leaned in, brushing his lips over the feathery crown of her head. "It will be fine. Don't worry."

She gave him a hesitant chirp as she bobbed her head. He was right.

In a few weeks, this curse would be no more. And then she could get to know him without being forced into a relationship due to a spell. She'd like that, a lot.

Kianso offered her another grape. He'd been a sweetheart about feeding her. She shook her head. "No thank you."

He plopped it onto his tongue and in a blink the orb vanished into his mouth. Oooh, she wished she were in human form so she could throw her arms around his neck and kiss the nectar from his delectable lips.

Her beak dropped open watching him. He stroked a knuckle along her throat. "What time is it?" she asked.

"Two thirty."

She dipped her head down. "Only two and a half hours to go."

He lifted her higher, so they were at eye level. "It will pass quickly, you'll see."

"Not quick enough," she replied. "Can we spend the evening at home tonight?"

"Sure. Do you have anything special in mind?" he asked with a wink.

"Naughty things. Very naughty things."

A laugh of approval rumbled in his chest, sending warmth all through her body. She may be in an avian form, but her reactions were one hundred percent human female.

Not to mention her jaguar shifter longed to purr and stretch beneath his capable hands.

Pandora approached at a near run, with her legs striking against the long skirt that she wore, causing the fabric to hitch up with every step she took. Charisma trailed a few steps behind her. As the two halted, Pandora unfolded a book from beneath her arm.

Sasha swallowed. The lump in her throat grew from a tiny seed to a heavy rock.

"Something's wrong. What's the matter?" she asked Pandora in a rush.

"Don't be alarmed, my dear. We're committed to helping you with whatever you need," Charisma began.

"You're scaring me," Sasha said.

"Just spit it out," Kianso urged.

Pandora opened the book, but Sasha thought it was more to stall than that she actually needed the tome.

"Marigold discovered an addendum to the spell. Apparently, in addition to being with your true love under Samhain's full moon, the person who decreed the curse must also be present and repeal the spell."

Sasha inhaled sharply. "Oh no. How will I convince her to come here? Lilly will never agree to that."

"You can't be certain, dear," Charisma said.

"I don't see how she would help me. She's the reason I'm in this mess," Sasha whispered, her voice trembling.

Pandora gently closed the book. "We have some time. I'm sure you'll think of something."

They were at the condo well before five o'clock. Sasha paced on the glass coffee table, the tips of her talons making clicking sounds as she traveled back and forth. As the switching hour arrived, she froze in anticipation.

Finally, a tiny hum began in her core and circled outward into her shoulders and limbs. Then she jumped into the air and landed on two feet, whole in her human form.

With her emotions in turmoil, she stretched both arms over her head, entwining them languidly before letting her hands fall and settle behind her head and then shoulders, exposing her heart to him. "I want…" She paused, capturing his gaze with hers. Could he tell what she needed…wanted? Her gaze slanted to the side. "Perhaps we should go to the bedroom."

He took three enormous steps forward and drew her up against him, pressing his hardness against her soft mound. She lifted her leg and wound it around his hips to his back. He helped her, lifting her leg higher still while at the same time sliding his palm beneath her bottom. A shimmer of electricity ran through her. She wrapped her arms around his neck and guided him closer until their lips locked in a fierce, hungry kiss.

"Yes. The bedroom," he said into her mouth as he lifted her into his strong arms.

12

Sasha opened her eyes an hour and a half later, coming down from the pleasure high to see Kianso, resting on his side with his head propped in his hand, watching her.

"You're beautiful," he said. His fingers smoothed a line down her neck, over her collar bone and shoulder, and skipped along her arm.

She stretched like the cat shifter she was, satisfied, happy, and bone-limp. "Mmm. You're talented."

He tipped his head down and kissed her. "Shall we go for round two?"

Abruptly she realized she'd forgotten about time. The one thing she so carefully monitored had totally left her brain. She placed a palm on his chest, pushing him away. "The time?"

She looked across his magnificent body as he fell back onto the mattress—a golden god, stretched out on the bed beside her—as her gaze darted to the bedside clock. Seven. Her stomach rumbled.

He rolled to his side of the bed and stood. "Okay. I'll go rustle us up some dinner while you shower. How does that sound?"

Sasha rose on the other side, dragging the sheet with her. She faced him, with the expanse of the bed between them, and marveled at how magnificent he looked standing there in all his naked glory. "Delicious." She smiled wickedly.

He raised a brow and the muscle in his jaw worked, as if he were fighting for control.

She gave a throaty laugh and then turned toward the bathroom, forcing herself not to glance back as she heard the swish of his clothes behind her.

A smorgasbord of leftovers greeted him when he opened the refrigerator. He took several boxes out and set them on the counter along with some plates. He would allow her to make her own selections and then reheat their food in the microwave. Not fancy, but it would work.

Sasha exited the bedroom with her chin-length hair damp and finger combed. She looked fantastic.

Their lovemaking had been impromptu and intense. He sensed her need to feel completely alive and connected. And he was glad he was there for her to turn to.

"I hope you're hungry. I think we have enough leftovers. The restaurants were very generous in the portions," he said.

"I think I've worked up an appetite."

He gave a low laugh. "Indeed."

She walked right into his open arms and kissed him. "Make your selections and I'll bring it to you."

She pointed to the Guillermo's boxes. "That'll do."

"Good. I'll have the same." He kissed her forehead. "How 'bout we eat in the living room?"

She nodded. "Okay."

He let go of her, even as his fingers itched to pull her back, and watched the enticing sway of her hips as she strolled to the sofa. Her fluid strides made him envision the feline shifter in her. She curled up on the leather couch to wait for him.

A few minutes later the ding of the microwave told him their dinner was warm and ready. Just like him. But there wouldn't be time for what he had on his mind. No, she needed her nourishment while she had the chance.

He made a tray for them, carried it into the living room, and took a seat beside her. She leaned curled up beside him while they ate. The sofa had been the perfect choice. Nothing in between them. Sasha draped one long leg over his.

When they finished eating, he set the containers aside and placed his arm around her shoulders. She rested her head against him. This is where he wanted her to stay, forever. Right by his side.

If only this dreadful curse were gone.

And what if Halloween came and they couldn't fix things? Then what? He tried to control his breathing so he wouldn't let on how much the thought tore him up inside.

"Thank you for today," she said huskily, and then she changed into a parrot right before his eyes.

He immediately placed his hand down for her to step upon and then set her on his chest. "You're welcome." He was quiet for several moments, thinking of the challenges before them, then said, "I have to go home tomorrow and back to work."

She didn't say anything, but turned her head away, looking out the window.

"Do you want to come with me, or stay here in Nocturne Falls?" He rushed on trying to sound unconcerned. "Whatever you choose, I can return on the weekends."

"I don't want to be a burden."

"You won't be. I work during the day. You are welcome to hang out wherever you choose."

"I don't know."

He wished he could read her better when she was in bird form.

She tilted her head. "Caroline has been so kind to take me in. She's used to dealing with all sorts of animals. It's not the same for you."

"Come home with me," he urged more adamantly. "I have a plan to get Lilly to Nocturne Falls for Halloween. Trust me."

13

He stared into the darkness as night fell, sipping his glass of bourbon and numbly tuning into the subtle flavors of orange, vanilla, and spice rolling over his tongue. It took two stiff drinks before he could relax enough to sleep. He remained on the couch. His memory kept returning to their romp in bed. She'd been so warm and responsive in his arms just hours earlier. He desired to have her in his arms right now. But he felt the distance growing between them with her uncertainty. And it made him nervous.

He stroked the parrot nesting on his chest. He would do everything in his power to help her find a way out of the spell. Then he could love her the way he wanted to, the way she deserved.

He dozed fitfully throughout the night; in his

mind he reviewed his plan, ready to put it into motion as soon as he got to his office. He was staring at the ceiling when the alarm he'd set on his cell phone chimed. Cupping her to his chest with one hand, he rose and punched the off button. She wriggled free and flew into the kitchen where she perched on the back of a stool.

"I've decided to go with you," she said, extending her wings. "If that's still okay."

"Of course it is. I was hoping you'd agree." He stood and stretched tired muscles, a jubilant mood washing over him. She was coming with him. Yes.

Tyler was a short hour-and-a-half ride from Nocturne Falls. Kianso had put up the topper on the car this morning because of the damp, misty weather. He drove straight to his office and arrived early, according to what he'd told her—in time to tackle what he'd planned for Lilly Reese before he began his appointments.

Sasha was skeptical and curious about his intentions. How could he possibly get Lilly to agree to come to Nocturne Falls? Her acceptance was the first step. The second was to get her to revoke the spell—yes, her cooperation would be the easiest solution—but beyond that, was there another way to undo the spell? Sasha sighed, not at all convinced Lilly would help her.

Her heartbeat thrummed against her ribs. Her eyes grew moist.

If things didn't work out, then she would disappear. It wasn't fair to entangle him in her strange half existence.

She wanted to believe him. Still, a tiny damaged part of her deep inside wondered if she could truly trust anyone.

With a deep breath, she regained her composure. She perched on Kianso's shoulder as he collected information from the internet. She recognized Lilly's address and phone number when he scrolled down the screen. "That's her," she bit out.

He grabbed the information. Then he typed a very official-looking letter declaring that Lilly was the winner of a five-day and four-night, all-expense-paid trip for two to Nocturne Falls over Halloween, October 28 through November 1.

"For two? That's mighty generous."

"She will be more likely to use the offer if she can bring a friend. Don't you think?"

"Yes. Smart thinking. All she has to do is get there. The drive from Montgomery to Nocturne Falls is nothing, less than four hours." She thought of her own trip nine months ago. It had taken her two days because of the curse. Since she was only in human form a short time each day, she'd had to split the driving time into two segments. Her car filled with the few things she'd brought was still parked at Caroline's house.

"I'm paying for this," she insisted.

"Hey, it's my idea. I'm offering up Seth's condo for them to stay at. I'm sure he won't mind. It's probably too late to find accommodations elsewhere."

"True. Okay. But I'm picking up all other tabs. Let's include three hundred dollars in food."

"That will be an added benefit." He smiled at her. "If you weren't a bird right now, I'd squeeze the daylights out of you."

"Hold that thought until this evening." She shot him a sideways glance, not at all sure her eyes conveyed the desire she felt.

Sasha pulled herself back to the task at hand and clamped her beak shut Would Lilly take the bait? She hoped so.

"What if she doesn't respond?"

"I'd hate to resort to plan B," he grumbled.

"What's that?"

He shrugged. "I'm not sure. Kidnap her perhaps."

"You can't do that." Even as she protested, she couldn't help the unbidden image of Lilly resting in the back seat of the Mustang with her hands and feet wrapped in duct tape. No, she couldn't do that even to people who had wronged her.

He glanced at her. "We'll see about that. We can do this the easy way, or the hard way. It's up to her."

She watched him, admiring the determination in his eyes. It was a side of him she hadn't seen, yet she liked a lot. She was touched that he was willing to go to such lengths to help her.

The final lines were the cherry on top. The instructions indicated a response must be received by October 20 or the offer would be forfeited. He listed his law firm's e-mail contact for a quicker response. Brilliant. That way they'd know if she planned on coming to town, or not.

Of course, there was always the possibility of her saying one thing and not following through...the tiny negative voice in the far corner of her brain chimed in. Pressing her lips together, she squashed it.

This would work. It had to, or else she'd be stuck in this limbo forever.

It was a grueling wait. For nine days, she helped Kianso check his mail and inbox, anticipating Lilly's reply. They were down to the deadline without an acceptance.

With every minute that passed, she grew more nervous.

They had gotten into a routine, playing house during her normal hours, with her keeping him company during the day at his office. Over the weekends they drove to Nocturne Falls. Today was Friday, so they were on their way.

He had arranged his schedule so that they drove during the mid-afternoon to Nocturne Falls. That put them in town at dinner hour when she could make the most of her three hours in human form.

She eyed the phone on the console between the seats where his cell phone rested in silence.

She sighed, transferring her focus outside the car. The skies were clear, the weather brisk, and the leaves on the trees had already turned orange and red. She tried to appreciate the gorgeous fall day. As they drove into town, with perfect scheduling, she changed into her human self. She stretched in the bucket seat and then lifted his phone to peer at it one more time, wondering if she'd missed the chime of an e-mail. Nothing.

She chewed on the corner of her last good fingernail. What were they going to do now?

"Staring at it won't make the mail happen," he said with far more lightness in his voice than she felt.

"I know." She placed her hand on his shoulder and leaned in, giving him a kiss on his cheek. "You've been wonderful. Thanks for helping me keeping my sanity."

"Is that all I've helped you with?" he teased.

A flush rushed into her cheeks. "Hmm. I *have* gotten rid of a lot of pent-up energy lately." She couldn't help but grin back at him.

He winked at her. And like that, her mood improved. The warm swish in her chest that she always got at his sexy smile filled her.

At Mummy's Diner, he parked, got out of the Mustang, and walked around to open the door for her. They had become Friday night regulars at the restaurant. He was motioning for her to enter when his phone chimed.

Sasha straightened, watching him as he looked at the screen. His eyes twinkled.

"What is it?" Her heart raced.

He rotated the phone around so she could read the message. *I'm thrilled to claim my prize. I will arrive in Nocturne Falls as indicated on October 28.*

She gave a little squeal and threw her arms around his neck. "You did it! Now if she doesn't back out or something—"

He placed a finger beneath her chin and lifted it, looking into her eyes. "Whatever happens, you're my true love. Always. We are meant to be together."

She gave him a half smile without saying a word because she didn't want to lie. She swallowed the peach pit-sized lump in her throat, all scratchy and painful. If this didn't work, then she would leave and allow him to get on with living a whole life.

14

Bedtime was the most difficult hour of the day. When he would have loved to hold Sasha curled up beside him, sleeping. And when his doubts stung as if he'd been caught in a school of box jellyfish in Hanauma Bay. He shivered at a memory.

He noticed that the closer they got to Halloween, the more hesitant Sasha became. It was as if she didn't want to trust too much, perhaps afraid the plan would fall through and she'd be stuck in this life forever.

He'd tried to reassure her that he wanted her no matter what the outcome. And yet, a barrier remained between them. Every time he mentioned he desired her even in her present state, she'd clammed up.

Somehow he needed to prove to her they could make a relationship work. That he loved her. He grinned to himself, acknowledging what he felt. Three weeks ago, when he'd accepted Seth's invite he had no way of knowing the big, wonderful changes heading his way. But at the same time, he knew, it had to be right for her also.

Now that he'd met Sasha, he didn't want to think of his life without her.

He shook his head. No, everything would work out fine. Hadn't his animal guides told him as much?

He closed his eyes, and as he slept, he ventured into the world of his shamanic calling.

They pulled into Caroline's drive on Friday a week later, the day before Lilly's scheduled arrival. This evening Sasha had requested a meeting with the Nocturne witchy sisters and they had been kind enough to agree. Sasha wanted to make sure she had all her bases covered. She would have only one chance to get everything right during the full moon on Halloween. Otherwise, according to Pandora, it would be another nineteen years before the conditions were right again.

Holy cats and dogs. She couldn't withstand a life in limbo for that long. She just couldn't.

"Where do you want me to put our things?" Kianso asked, entering the foyer.

"The guest room is on the left," Sasha said, pointing the way. Caroline had welcomed them as guests through Halloween, or for as long as they needed. As predicted, all accommodations within forty-five miles were sold out.

"Thank you for letting us stay here," Sasha said.

"Yes. It was very nice of you. Thanks," Kianso added.

"Glad to have you," Caroline replied. "I set bath towels on the bed. Make yourselves at home."

"Got it," Sasha said. "Same as before."

They set their things in the bedroom and then prepared to greet Pandora and her sisters. Actually, they weren't positive who would be stopping by to help them, but she appreciated any and all of their help.

They had broken their multiweek Friday streak of eating at Mummy's, but not completely. Tonight they'd stopped on the way into town and grabbed enough takeout for guests. Sasha arranged the food on the dinette table along with some spiced apple cider.

Kianso scooped dip onto a nacho chip and plopped it into his mouth. He strolled over to Sasha and encircled her with his strong arms. "No matter what happens, I'm here for you."

Sasha held tight to the overwhelming feelings

sparking through her chest. She was thankful for his support. And there was a part of her that wanted more from him, much more. If only they had a normal relationship.

The doorbell rang.

Caroline did the honors of opening the front door. Pandora, Charisma, and Marigold strolled in single file.

"Thank you so much for meeting with us this evening," Sasha said.

"We're glad to help, child," Pandora replied.

Charisma headed straight to the food and plucked a fried mushroom from a tray. "You even have Mummy's Better-Than-Sex Pie! I like your style, girlie."

"Help yourself to some snacks. Then Kianso will fill you in on what's happening," Sasha said. "Caroline, you too." She didn't want her friend to feel left out, especially since she'd been on her side since she arrived in Nocturne Falls.

Everyone filled a plate and then found a seat in the living room. Kianso sat beside Sasha on the love seat with his arm around her shoulders. The feeling of support in the room boosted her confidence. She was too nervous to eat, but she sipped on a glass of cider.

"Okay," Kianso began. "Lilly Reese is in town. We offered her a 'free' trip here for Halloween and she accepted. So, half our task is accomplished."

"How clever. And you didn't have to resort to force, because that would have never worked," Pandora said.

"Good," Charisma chimed in. "We need three elements to revoke the spell." She read from a book. "A remorseful heart, a true love's start, beneath a magical moon, bears a healing boon."

Sasha considered what Charisma had read. "Who has to be remorseful? Lilly?"

"Yes. The person who cast the spell has to regret what they'd done," Pandora said.

"I doubt she's sorry," Sasha said.

"Maybe Lilly simply needs a bit of guidance," Marigold said. She leaned over and patted the back of Kianso's hand. "You love her, don't you?"

Sasha almost spewed her drink all over the place. She swallowed quickly and coughed to recover from the bit of liquid she'd inhaled.

Kianso took her hand in his as he stared into her eyes. "Yes, I love her."

"Then everything should work out fine," Marigold chuckled.

Sasha wondered why the witch hadn't asked her if she loved him. Could Marigold see her love for Kianso even though Sasha hadn't been willing to voice it? She sucked the flesh of her cheek in between her teeth and toyed with it. Somewhere deep within she didn't feel she deserved his love. And she was guarding herself against disappointment.

As if reading her mind, Pandora waved her hand at Sasha. "We know you love him."

Kianso raised a brow and peered at Sasha. "Do you now?"

She leaned in close enough for her breath to mingle with his. "Yes," she whispered, and then brushed her lips over his. "Okay, let's return to the subject of saving my backside."

"I do like your backside."

Charisma cleared her throat. "On Halloween at seven thirty we'll all meet at the fountain. We'll work the spell reversal then."

Pandora nodded. "Just make sure Lilly is there with you."

15

Kianso had included his phone number and instructions in the acceptance e-mail he'd sent Lilly Reese, so on Saturday, he'd been expecting her call when she arrived in town. He and Sasha had decided it would be best for him to handle the details of her stay and for Sasha to remain on the sideline until Halloween. That way they might be able to gauge the likelihood of Lilly being willing to free her of the curse.

After filling in the Excelsior staff about the "prize winners," Kianso greeted Lilly and her male guest at the front door. "Ms. Reese?" he inquired, as she strutted through the double doors the valet and the man were holding open for her.

"Yes. Hello."

"Welcome to Nocturne Falls. I'm Kianso Kane, of the Kane law office."

"Pleased to meet you. This is James Gibson."

Kianso took in the petite woman with curly, dark-red hair. She was much shorter than Sasha, and had big blue-gray eyes. James sported a dark beard. Tattoos disappeared into the T-shirt sleeves of both arms.

"I don't know how I was so lucky to win a trip." Her laugh came out with a little snort.

"I have a welcome packet for you." He held out a folder emblazoned with his law office name and logo, and then opened it for her to see the contents. "Here is the key to the condo. This elevator will take you to the fourth floor. Plus, you will find gift cards to most of the Nocturne Falls restaurants and a few boutiques. This is a five-thousand-dollar value. All you have to do is enjoy the holiday festivities and stay through November first."

"I have to stay over Halloween?" Her voice turned whiny and uncertain.

"Yes. That's required in the package," Kianso said firmly.

She turned her head to look at James. "That means we'll miss the big bash at the ranch." She thrust out her bottom lip and glanced at Kianso. "I really hadn't decided if we'd stay the entire time."

"You won't find a better Halloween celebration than here in Nocturne Falls." He figured that was indeed the case since they celebrated the holiday continually. And this year he'd find out firsthand.

Lilly gave a hesitant nod. "I guess."

"Good." He handed her the electronic key and packet. "Enjoy your stay."

As if a switch had been flipped, she turned all bubbly. Stepping toward the elevator, she said, "This is going to be so fun!"

Kianso waved. "See you around."

In her bird form, Sasha watched from outside the building. She couldn't hear the conversation, but observed the play of emotions changing on Lilly's face. Her old friend was a drama queen, for sure. It was a quality that drove Sasha crazy sometimes. That, and Lilly changed opinions like a chameleon changed colors.

But Lilly's biggest weakness was men. Sasha had felt a twinge of unease as Kianso conversed with the woman. She reminded herself that Lilly was a witch who couldn't be trusted. That alone made her nervous.

Feeling a buzz glide over her feathers, she changed into her human self as Kianso strolled up to her. "That wasn't the same man she was with when she put the hex on me," she said, her voice sounding somewhat bitter.

"You mean I can't sock him for coming on to you?"

She grinned. He was trying to lighten her mood and make her relax. It worked. She slid her arms around his waist and gazed up into his eyes. "Everything go okay?"

"Yes." There was a hesitation in his voice.

"But...?" she questioned.

He shrugged. "I have a hard time reading her."

"Now you see how I ended up in this predicament. I thought she was my friend."

"Have you spoken to her since she put the spell on you?"

"No."

"Maybe's she's sorry."

"I don't know. Perhaps." She put her cheek on his chest. "Lilly is caught up in her own fantasies. She acts before she thinks. Everything depends on her frame of mind when I ask her to rescind the curse. I figure I have a fifty-fifty chance."

"Better than nothing," he added.

"Yes, it is. I can hope."

He smoothed his hand over her hair to the back of her neck and looked deeply into her eyes. "Have faith."

Halloween fell on a Tuesday this year. Saturday turned into Sunday. Sunday turned into Monday.

They were the longest, most tormenting three days of her life.

Kianso had taken her out and tried to entertain her, but she constantly looked over her shoulder and kept an eye out in case they crossed paths with Lilly. Part of her was relieved she didn't see her old friend. Another part wanted to get on with the business of confronting her.

"It's not time for us to tip our hand, love."

"I know you're right," she responded.

At last, Halloween evening arrived. Sasha paced inside the Hallowed Bean. She wore a Cleopatra costume. She'd chosen it because of the Egyptian ruler's fondness for leopards. Kianso dressed as Mark Antony. They made a handsome couple. Everyone in the streets tonight would be dressed for Halloween, even the humans. The entire town was charmed by the biggest party she'd ever seen.

Sasha sipped a steamy caramel macchiato, trying to allow the sweet creamy drink to melt away her worries. After the sun set, the air had turned quite chilly. She sighed as the warm liquid trickled down her throat. But even the delicious drink did little to calm her. She glanced at the clock on the wall, a thought occurring to her. "You haven't talked to Lilly, have you? How are you going to get her to the meeting place?"

He held up his phone.

"You're relying totally on calling her?"

"Not exactly. There was a special ticket in her packet to be exchanged tonight by the fountain. I texted her earlier today to remind her of it." He grinned.

"Well, put cheese on my taters." She punched his shoulder, and then fell into his waiting arms. "For a second I panicked."

"I know." He hugged her and kissed the top of her head. "It's time. We should be leaving."

She stepped back, straightening. "I'm ready."

Out on the street, Main had been blocked off from traffic. The businesses were set up for trick-or-treaters and children toted special Nocturne Falls trick-or-treat bags. Special effects had been set up with black lights and strobe lighting and fog machines. Places like the Hallowed Bean offered spooky sound effects.

The vampires and werewolves and different creatures of Nocturne Falls interacted with the spectators, giving them an awesome show. This was Halloween on steroids. Sasha strolled down the street at Kianso's side, marveling at the creativity.

They arrived at the fountain early to discover Lilly and James already there.

Sasha halted abruptly, her feet scraping on the sidewalk.

Lilly's head turned.

For a moment, Sasha's heart beat in her ears.

Then, Lilly let out a happy squeal and ran, closing the distance between them. Sasha blinked her eyes, not quite believing what seemed to be transpiring. Lilly appeared glad to see her.

Lilly clutched Sasha's hands in hers. "I can't believe you're here. I looked for you after…after."

It seemed as if Lilly couldn't quite admit what she'd done. Then she held out her hand and ring finger. "Look. James just asked me to marry him. Isn't that wonderful?"

Left somewhat dumbfounded, Sasha peered at the ring on Lilly's finger. "Yes. Congratulations. That's fabulous."

Lilly inhaled a gigantic breath and stepped back, glancing around as Pandora, Charisma, Marigold, and Caroline joined the group. Comprehension flitted in her eyes that something was going on. Then her gaze shot to Kianso. "What is this?" She reached her hand out for James to take and offer her support. He did.

Kianso put an arm around Sasha's shoulders.

"My life has been a mess, because of the spell you put on me."

"I'm sorry. So sorry," Lilly said. "I tried to find you when I realized what I'd done. But you were gone."

"A spell cast in anger needs to be set right," Pandora said.

"We're here to help," Marigold chimed in.

"I don't know how to undo it," Lilly admitted. "I did some research, but my resources weren't enough."

Charisma lifted the book she held. "We have the answers. Right here."

"You just have to be willing to help," Sasha said.

Lilly stared at them; her eyes widened and then they dipped with shame. "I am. What do you need me to do?"

A rush of air escaped Sasha. *This just might work.* She felt Kianso squeeze her shoulder.

"Gather in closer, people," Pandora ordered. "Charisma, the book, please."

Sasha was glad the witches took charge. Pandora waved a wand over the book and spoke the same words she did before. "A remorseful heart, a true love's start, beneath a magical moon, bears a healing boon."

Sasha tilted her head back, staring at the huge, orange moon. A once every nineteen years moon. And it was shining on her tonight. Pandora repeated the phrase. "A remorseful heart, a true love's start, beneath a magical moon, bears a healing boon."

Nothing seemed to be happening. Her gaze sliced to Kianso. What did that mean? Was he not her true love? Did she not love him? Oh yes, she did. She captured his face between her hands. "I love you," she told him in a voice so soft, only he could hear.

"A remorseful heart, a true love's start, beneath a magical moon, bears a healing boon."

On the third repetition, Sasha's knees buckled. She blacked out.

Kianso caught Sasha before she completely crumpled to the ground. He lifted her, adjusting her weight in his arms. "Sasha. What's happening?" He appealed to Pandora.

The hawk spirit guide landed on a lamp post saying, "It's okay, brother."

Kianso allowed air into his lungs, relieved his spirit guides were watching over them.

"It's the spell leaving her body. She'll be fine," Charisma explained.

"Sasha." He leaned over her, checking her breathing. When her chest rose and fell, he relaxed a fraction. Then he turned and sat on the lip of the fountain, so he could better cradle her on his lap. "Sasha. Love. Wake up."

She blinked open her eyes. "The moon. Isn't that the most beautiful thing you've ever seen?"

Kianso didn't even glance up. "No. You're the most beautiful thing I've ever seen in my life."

She drew hands up around his neck. "What time is it?"

"Eight o-four."

A smile spread across her face and danced in her eyes. "The spell is broken." She pulled him down to kiss her.

"Come on gals, our job is done," Pandora said, turning. "And you, missy"—she pointed at Lilly—"I hope you visit Nocturne Falls another time. We all make mistakes. Just don't let it happen again." She gave a sharp nod.

"I'm glad he tricked me into coming." Lilly stepped closer to Kianso, and shoved his shoulder. "But next time just ask."

Kianso sat precariously on the edge of the fountain, supporting Sasha's weight in his arms. Lilly's push sent him off kilter. In an effort to keep from falling sideways, he overcompensated and toppled backward into the fountain, still holding Sasha and allowing her to settle on him.

She pushed up, laughing, shaking off water.

They all joined in the laughter. "Now that you've had a Nocturne Falls christening, you'll never leave," Pandora said.

"That's fine with us," Sasha spoke up.

Kianso grinned. He liked the way the word *us* rolled off her tongue. "Yes, that's fine with us," he repeated, then kissed several water droplets from her cheek and lips. Rising to his feet, he extended his hand and helped her out of the fountain.

He leaned in, saying in her ear, "Let's go home and take a shower."

"Where's home?" Sasha asked.

"Caroline's place for tonight," he replied.

Pandora stopped walking and looked over her shoulder. "I can help you with that problem." She handed Kianso her real estate business card. "Stop by my office."

Kianso grasped Sasha's hand and winked. "We definitely will."

Want more?

In this story, you met Seth, the archangel from the Divine Tree Guardian series. Discover more about Seth and the Immortal Guardians in AWAKENING FIRE, a story set in Tyler, Georgia, just a short drive from Nocturne Falls. Turn the page to read an excerpt!

Discover more about Larissa's books at www.larissaemerald.com.

Thank you for reading *Under the Nocturne Moon*. If you enjoyed these stories and want to stay up-to-date on my upcoming books, giveaways, and release dates, then sign up for my newsletter. (I promise your e-mail address will never be shared and you can unsubscribe at any time.)

https://larissaemerald.wordpress.com/contact/

Excerpt from

AWAKENING FIRE
THE DIVINE TREE GUARDIAN SERIES

BY LARISSA EMERALD

1

At the subterranean entrance to the Divine Tree sanctuary, Venn Hearst halted and raised his eyes to the etchings of a wolf and hawk emblazoned in the aged wood above the door, a nod to his alternate forms. Venn extended his tattooed wrist, positioning the elaborately inked tree, and the pulsing artery beneath it, below a glistening twisted root for the anointing ritual. An amber-colored drop of sap spilled over the image, then pooled and bubbled before it was absorbed into his skin, sending a sharp zing to each of his neurons before settling within the larger matching tat on his back.

The language of the universe rustled through

the air. The Secrets men died to know, Guardians swore to protect, and the Dark Realms were determined to steal or destroy were housed within this sacred place.

His Divine Tree was one of the original dozen hidden around the globe. There were eleven left after the Divine Tree Guardians had lost his brother Euler along with the Divine Tree in Germany in the mid-nineteen hundreds. The tree's demise had caused the earth to shift on its axis ever so slightly, bringing them one step closer to Armageddon with an escalation of malevolent forces. Evil had blossomed with Hitler taking millions of lives before balance could be restored. It had been an uphill battle ever since.

Venn opened and closed his fist, considering the tattoo on his wrist. Not even one more tree could be lost.

"Benison," the oak whispered.

"Blessings," Venn returned. "My strength and loyalty are yours."

With his vow, the door to the tree creaked opened, and he strode through the massive entry. He looked around the comfortable aboveground chambers and kept walking. Keeping watch wasn't his intention this night. No, he sought the tombs within the root structure below and hoped the tree would communicate to him if something out of the ordinary was happening.

He grabbed a nearby flashlight from the alcove next to the door, flipped it on, and started along the narrow tunneled path, down a staircase that had been fashioned by twisted knots of wood and roots fused together over centuries. It wound deep into the layers of knowledge, to the catacomb of interconnected scripts, like a true, living computer.

Once in the belly, he ran a hand over an electrical switch. Battery powered lights illuminate the cave-like room in a pale glow. Venn glanced about and drew an awed breath. *Holy shit. The place had grown.*

With careful steps, he moved from the tunnel into a cavern, where rough splinters jutted out of smooth swirls in the timber's pattern, creating a golden wooden cave. He used to come down here often in the beginning, during the early years of loneliness, always expecting to discover something exceptional. Which he usually did.

He'd learned that if he pricked himself on this special wood, a series of images would fire though his brain, teaching him something new, its lessons sharper and more thorough than those of any history or science channel on TV.

Centuries ago, he'd stumbled on this cavern and its amazing phenomenon quite by accident. The power the tree gave him had become an obsession, the data exchange an addiction. He knew better than to come back again after that. But this time he had no choice, his duty demanded he use every means available to him. He was well aware of the risks and didn't intend to overstep his limits.

Something was off-kilter in the universe, and he needed to know why. The odd weather pattern—winter when it should be spring—was an ominous sign, Venn knew, even if humans simply took it as a fluke of nature. Just as humans showed symptoms of illness, so too did the machinations of the universe. And a shift between good and evil often triggered such nasty weather patterns.

He needed to be on high alert. "Custos," he spoke quietly to the ancient tree. "Do you know what's going on?"

There was no answer.

Taking a seat in a worn cradle of wood, he felt the need to connect with the Divine Tree…and to his brothers. He squeezed the back of his neck. Perhaps that's what the problem was. Not outside at all, but within him.

He felt as isolated from everything as this tree was. What was it like to house all humanity but not feel humanity?

The groan and creak of the tree, as if it were caught by a strong gust of wind, caused Venn to lift his head. Seth stood framed in the tunnel doorway. "I didn't think you'd be down here," the angel said, walking into the chamber.

Now Venn *knew* there was trouble brewing. The

angel rarely dropped in just to say hello. "What's happenin'?" Venn asked in way of greeting.

Seth shrugged, his wings lifting and falling with the movement. "I'm not sure. But you must feel it also if you're down here."

"Indeed. Have a seat," Venn motioned to another curve of wood.

Seth sat and crossed his legs, resting his back and folded wings against the smooth inner walls of the tree. "I dunno. On one hand the off weather pattern seems like a trivial thing, but coupled with all the unrest in the world—with ISIS beheading people in the Middle East and people protesting over police in the US—I think we need to pay close attention."

"I agree. The planet is digressing into a state of anarchy and I'd bet my right arm that the Dark Realm is behind it all," Venn proclaimed.

"No doubt."

"I think you'd better hang around," Venn suggested.

"Fine. You got a room to spare?" Seth asked, firing a glance from beneath heavy eyelids without lifting his head.

"No."

Seth shrugged. "Then I can't help you."

Venn chuckled, knowing full well he'd just gained a house guest. "It's hard to think back to when this guardianship began." He rested his head back and closed his eyes, trying to see that far into the past. "You know you could have given us a little more information when you set us on this task."

"What for? You figured it out."

"Huh. It took me forever to learn to control my shifting. The hawk being able to manipulate time and space, and the wolf's incredible strength. Shit, I was a mess in those days."

"You're still a mess," said with exaggerated disdain.

Venn straightened. "Hey, I didn't ask for this gig. You can head back up anytime."

+ % =

Emma sympathized with anyone who had to make transatlantic flights on a regular basis. The trip from Paris to Atlanta's Hartsfield–Jackson airport had left her weary as a rag doll. Two hours later, she was still stifling yawns as she surveyed the snow-covered park where her mélange-metal statue would reside.

"I'm sorry. I shouldn't have made you stop here on the way from the airport. You must be exhausted." Grams tugged the zipper of her trendy black leather jacket higher before passing the leash attached to her little, aging Yorkshire terrier, Izzy, from one hand to the other. The pup scooted around her legs. "It was thoughtless of me. I'm just so excited."

Emma shrugged. "I'm fine," she assured her grandmother, then twisted to face the trunk of the enormous tree they stood beneath when the next yawn came. A whisper of energy coiled around her, heat seeming to seep out of the bark itself. She pursed her mouth and clasped her arms around her rib cage. As if the move offered any protection. Fatigue always made her paranoid. She even sometimes saw visions, though she didn't like to admit it, even to herself.

She sighed. No use in worrying about something she couldn't control, and she'd long since learned she wasn't in the driver's seat where her visions were concerned. Instead, she engaged in her most prevalent form of evasion, her art.

Nothing wrong with burying problems in a little work.

She studied the space again. Which metals would capture the hues of oyster shells in the sky? What subject would best fit the colors? Emma jotted down some mental notes for her next project. She watched the changing colors of dusk descend on the park as clouds loomed, back-lit in an eerie coppery shimmer. The diffused light made the snow appear almost warm, the rocks somehow spongy, and the trees… They were mystical.

Her apprehension escalated as the walkway in front of her blurred. Her knees grew weak.

No. Not this time.

She sucked in a deep breath and tensed, resisting. But she knew with sickening certainty that the vision was coming. There was no controlling it…

An arrow shaft protruded from her chest, and air wheezed through her stagnant lungs. In the wake of the brutal, radiating pain, time slowed. Her heart stopped.

Oh God.

An image of a huge gray wolf materialized, howling a cry of grief alongside her lifeless body, and it lingered, dimming slowly to a sepia shadow. Had she…died here?

Emma blinked, disoriented, as the brief manifestation faded, reality setting back in. Exhaling hard, she shifted her feet, peering down at her strappy, crystal-embellished, leopard-print sandals and seeking solid ground. Izzy licked at her toes where they peeked from her shoes, as if trying to console her as best he could.

Her gaze swept up her own body, and she settled shaky fingers over her beating heart. No blood. No arrow. Definitely alive.

Still, the suffocating sensation of a collapsed lung remained, causing her stomach to churn. How she even knew what one felt like alarmed her.

Stop thinking about it.

With determined strength, Emma overcame the pervasive mental intrusion, forcing her attention back to the grossly neglected Georgia park where she stood trembling, to the place her sculpture would call home. She'd had these dreams and visions her whole life, and when she'd researched the phenomenon, she'd discovered they were each giving her a glimpse of one of her past lives. If one believed in that sort of thing. Which she did. But knowing that didn't make it any less disturbing.

Emma's breath swirled in a misty cloud as she focused on her surroundings. Cold, damp air patted her cheeks. The massive oak before her released a sad moan. Or was that just her active imagination at work? Whatever it was triggered a familiar warmth that spread into her limbs, and reminded her she possessed...talents beyond her visions. Heat radiated through her right arm, and she glanced down, opening her blazing hot fist to discover she'd inadvertently melted her grandmother's butterfly key fob beyond recognition.

Some *talents*. More like she'd been cursed.

With an unsteady sigh, she pushed her hair away from her face. Geez, her life hadn't changed one iota. Since she was a toddler, she'd been molding metal with her bare hands as if it were clay, both intentionally and accidentally. It was the latter that caused her grief. The episode with a neighborhood boy and his squished red Hot Wheels car came to mind. It always did. Her dad had been so angry with her.

"Are you okay?"

Her grandmother's question snapped her back to the present. Would Grams know if she lied? She'd discovered when she'd moved to New York that the visions and dreams had lessened with the distance. She'd run all the way to Paris to avoid them. And they must have let go, too, because she hadn't thought of them for a long, long while.

"Sure. But I can't say the same for this." She dangled the key chain in the air.

Her grandmother gave a chuckle. "I should have nicknamed you Hot Hands."

Emma managed to summon a smile, but it faltered as her gaze shifted back to that tree. Its spindly canopy of branches seemed to reach out. The hair on her arms prickled. Something in the fractures of time yanked free and another ripple of unease washed over her.

Good and evil used this place as a playground. At the moment, evil acted the bully. She felt a bizarre tug-of-war for dominance, the power of it making her sway.

Leave. Me. Alone.

This evening's vision was beyond vivid—a seven-point-five on the Richter scale, and it wasn't passing as it normally did. She flailed her arms, trying to shake off her frustration. She usually had an easier time coming out of it. An erratic pulse thumped in her neck, bringing her circulation back. Her temples ached with the awakening.

212

She shook her head. *Ignore. Regroup. Move on.*

Thank goodness her grandmother, who tarried a few steps behind, wouldn't know the depth of Emma's latest episode, since time distorted or elongated only within her mind. What she needed was an anchor, physically and mentally. There was no way she'd allow her father to be right about her differences making her crazy. She didn't have a psychotic disorder as he'd suggested when she was young. No, she would control the visions, but, darn, this bout threatened her common sense. She'd never seen herself die before.

Besides, wasn't that supposed to kill you or something?

Or was that just in dreams, not visions? She gave a mental shrug, figuring it didn't matter because she had both.

Focus. She was here on a job. The park.

It was spring in Tyler, Georgia, yet the late-season snow masked the evidence. Weeds and yellow wildflowers nudged aside a layer of snow, and fresh green growth attempted to unfurl on branches. The square must have been lovely at one time, especially when everything began to bloom, but not now. A battered, rotten wood bench lay on the ground sideways, collapsed. The sidewalk that wound through the center of the park resembled a war zone, with chunks of concrete broken and upended. The branches of the old oak swept the earth. Clearly ignored for many, many years, the mammoth tree looked as if it had never been pruned or shaped.

The untamed tree was so out-of-character for prim-and-proper Georgia. Just like her. Her dad had always proclaimed that her overactive imagination would lead to trouble. If he only knew the whole truth.

A hand slid across Emma's back and bony fingers grasped her shoulder. She almost jumped out of her grandmother's hug.

"Just think, a Grant getting the honor of creating a statue for the old town square. I can hardly believe it." Grams heaved one of her exaggerated, bursting-with-pride sighs, the way she did when the family dinner table was landscaped to perfection.

"You drive a hard bargain, Grams. The committee couldn't say no." And neither could Emma. Her grandmother had requested a sculpture of a confederate soldier on a rearing horse. Not very original, but Emma had obliged, thankful for both the much-needed income and the chance to build her portfolio. She gradually relaxed into the woman's solid embrace, somewhat grounded again.

She touched her head to her grandmother's salon-teased auburn one, in the same let's-stick-together way she'd done since she was six, when she'd spent every summer vacation here after her family had moved to New York.

"Thanks for your help," Emma said. Nothing like getting paid to visit her favorite relative. Since the city had commissioned her sculpture for the park renovation project, she'd be hanging out for the next few weeks to supervise its placement and participate in the dedication ceremony.

Grams nodded. "Anytime. Paris is too darn far away, if you ask me." She picked Izzy up and tucked him beneath her arm.

Actually, the greater distance meant fewer visions, so it wasn't even far enough. Emma wasn't sure why, but they seemed to be worse, more frequent, when she returned to her Georgia birthplace. Bonus points for Paris.

"We talk and Skype all the time," Emma pointed out.

"That's not the same as seeing your smiling face." Her grandmother slid a hand down Emma's arm and back up over her shoulder. "Look at you. You're shivering."

Ominous gray clouds were moving in, and the sky was growing darker. Emma felt more than saw the clump of wet red clay that oozed into her Sam Edelman sandals. She tamped her foot against a rock to clear it. "What an awful spring. Can't believe it snowed on Easter."

"Yes. The pecan blooms froze. The crop'll be

ruined." A smile lit Grams's eyes, and she tsked, seeming to dismiss the unfortunate prediction that might steal her pocket money. "But give it a few days. It'll warm up."

"I'll hold you to that."

Tree branches whipped one way, then the other, generating an eerie whistling. Emma shuddered, then tugged the neckline of her suddenly constricting turtleneck sweater as she turned to explore a staked-out plot of ground. "It looks like this is where they plan to put the statue."

Her gaze swept along the snow-patched ground, up the broken walkway, to the side of the park where fluorescent-orange construction fencing sectioned off individual trees, marking them for protection. Landscaping equipment near the road formed a neat line, ready to be put to use.

A tiny ping caught in her gut, and her internal compass gravitated to the old oak standing center stage. Its trunk stretched out to the size of a small house, as if several trees had grown together. She frowned as intense golden eyes seemed to peer at her from the grained bark. A figment of her imagination? With her history, it had to be.

When the eyes vanished, she angled her head, unable to shake the weird drag on her heart. As if she should know something important, yet couldn't bring it forth. The feeling didn't seem like a remnant of her vision but felt like it originated from an entirely different source. More like an unfathomable power or presence. She scanned the park and rubbed her chilled arms, but she didn't see a single soul.

Io slipped behind the downed bulldozer bucket, in predator mode, his eyes fixed on his target: Emma Grant. The machine inched to the side as his back jammed against a metal support. In his eagerness, he hadn't sufficiently controlled his brute strength. He grumbled at the oversight but kept tuned to the young woman. While in human form, as he was now, his senses were faulty. It was a weak form, practically useless, with few special powers.

He'd known the moment Emma Grant had set foot on Georgia soil.

Not such a difficult task, really. He'd been expecting her.

Now, he was curious about the reason she'd stopped at the park on her way from the airport. Was the Divine Tree's power already blooming in Emma? Had the old tree spoken to her?

He'd met her quite by accident years ago when she was a little girl of five. They were in an ice cream shop, and he'd accidentally dropped a handful of coins on the floor—as fine motor skills was another issue he had with the human form. But it turned into a fortunate event for him, really, for Emma gathered the coins up off the floor. And to her great embarrassment, when she handed them back to him the lot was fused together in a solid clump of metal.

He knew then and there that she was gifted. And he made it his business to discover why. Eavesdropping in on her dreams at night gave him the connection to her past. Even over the years after she moved from Tyler, he managed to keep track of her. He was damned proud of himself for discovering the reason behind her metal-altering ability.

Well, it wasn't precisely *his* discovery, but he would take credit for it nonetheless.

When he'd killed Emma in her past life and she'd lain on the grassy ground with his arrow jutting out of her chest, her blood had seeped into this magical oak's roots. Who knew such a simple act would create the catalyst to destroy a Divine Tree? He certainly hadn't. Not until the High Counsel of Devils had recently congratulated him for it, that is. And he wasn't disappointed.

That arrow, her blood, and her reincarnation had caused a shift, something even he couldn't grasp the implications of. It had taken him shitloads of long, painful, boring hours of watching before he discovered how he could use her newborn alchemist powers to his advantage. He deserved this boon, and the recognition from the counsel. He'd show his brother, Seth, that he was equally as favored by his superiors.

Now if only he could overcome the free will part of the equation. He couldn't force her into using her alchemist powers on the metal as he wanted her to. At least not physically.

But there were other ways to get the results he desired.

With a mental shake, he glared at Emma.

Did she realize the connection she shared with the tree? If so, he'd have to move much more quickly than he'd thought. No, no, he wouldn't allow things to get out of hand. He swiped a restless hand along his jaw.

He tried to quiet the nervous energy that continually tugged him in conflicting directions. One moment he was certain of his mission's success, the next of its failure. His gaze darted from Emma to Mrs. Busybody, listening intently. He plunged his hands into his pockets, withdrew them, then clasped them behind him.

The best he could determine, Emma was simply cold, not agitated or suspicious.

And Mrs. Grant took credit for arranging the commission of the statue her granddaughter had arrived to install.

Yes, it was better that Emma thought her grandmother was the instigator. Better she not discover the significance of the invitation to the installation ceremony. At least not until the ruination of the tree was complete or Emma and the Guardian were dead. Either outcome would give him great pleasure.

After all, he'd discovered firsthand that the best way to make someone suffer was to destroy the one thing that someone most loved. Yes, revenge would be his. About time.

Seth, Mr. Goodie-Goodie, would soon have his world turned upside down. And Venn and the Divine Tree along with him. He could barely contain his excitement. Three for the price of one. Brilliant.

Excited and restless, Io tugged on his shirt sleeve, then sought focus by touching the picture of a burned tree he kept tucked in his pocket. It represented his brother's failure. His channeled hatred grew, and his smokescreen, the shield he'd put in place so the tree wouldn't detect his presence, disintegrated. Damn.

The stupid dog in the old lady's arms barked and growled.

A deep moan resounded within the catacomb. *Custos?* Venn straightened from his relaxed position. Immediately, his attention shot upward—

above him, outside—and he stood.

What *was* that?

An irresistible tug made him palm his chest. He proceeded through the cavern entrance, back up the knotted stairs and angled tunnel, the pull intensifying with each step. If he were human, he'd be wondering if he were having a heart attack.

He hadn't felt this collision of energy in two centuries.

Inside the sprawling tree, he climbed rough-hewn stairs to the watch room at ground level. He ignored the enormous circular space and its new modular furnishings as he fixed his attention on the highly polished wooden wall, where the force ran strongest. The bark itself had sight, a transparency by which he could see through the layers of wood to the world beyond, at will. He looked out, as he had done so many thousands of times in the past.

Outside, two females engaged in conversation. He immediately recognized Claire Grant. The old lady had been bragging everywhere she went about how her granddaughter, Emma, had designed a sculpture for Tyler's historic town square and oldest park.

Venn's park, not the town's.

But he'd lost that battle a long time ago, and until recently, he had managed to direct the city officials' attentions elsewhere. Damn their renewed interest. The tree had been marked for preservation purposes, which was a good thing, yet it also attracted unwanted attention. There were others who had an inclination of the riches the tree held, not in monetary value but in what they could do with the knowledge contained within.

The presumed granddaughter turned.

Venn advanced to the barrier, curious. He wanted to be closer to her, wanted nothing between them, not this tree, not this space. With his extraordinary sight and hearing, he could make her out perfectly, but it wasn't enough. There was something about her…yet he couldn't fathom why he'd be drawn to Claire Grant's granddaughter. How odd.

With a sweeping glance, the young woman arched her brows and strolled toward the tree. She seemed to stare right at him. Thick auburn hair draped over her shoulders, and she tilted her head, his equilibrium shattering. A roar took up residence inside his skull. Thunder vibrated through his chest, and explosive desire made him hard and ready.

His breath hitched. His inner beasts stirred without the customary summons, fighting each other, wolf and hawk vying for a glimpse of her.

She inched forward.

Yes, move closer.

She spoke, and he vaguely caught her whispered French phrase. *"Coeur de mon coeur."*

Heart of my heart.

He swallowed, hard.

She placed a delicate palm on the trunk, and Venn growled as a surge of energy—her very essence—flowed into the tree, filled him as much as earthy air filled his lungs.

"I...feel something," Emma said with opened-mouth awe. "The oak has been here for hundreds of years."

When recognition hit Venn, it was with the force of an 18-wheeler rear-ending a car waiting at a traffic light. Every muscle in his body tensed as he saw flashes of her in a past life, of their limbs entwined, of her lips warm on his, of her vibrant laugh...of her dying.

Could it truly be Amelia? Had she returned to him in this woman, this Emma Grant?

Venn closed his eyes and summoned energy in all its manifested forms—heat, light, sound, magnetism, gravity, and all of life's functions—reaching out to her, touching deep into her soul to test the theory. Her initial response was a lazy yawn, but then her mystical imprint danced, the spirit unique to her, proclaimed, *Yes!*

She. Was. His.

A heaviness slammed against his chest, followed by whiplash, pain, confusion. He'd been robbed of time, his woman, his love.

Ah, Amelia. Brought back to him after so long.

A spark flared in his chest, and his pulse sped

up. Unwilling to move lest this sudden feel-good moment disappeared, he held his breath.

She glanced over her shoulder at her grandmother. "I have the strangest feeling of déjà vu."

Overwhelmed, he wished he could vault through the barrier and take her in his arms. Instead, he braced both hands on thick chair arms as he slowly lowered himself into the seat, not taking his eyes off the woman with fiery hair and golden skin. Every fiber in his body stretched out to embrace her. She was his.

They'd been lovers in 1809. Companions. Promised journey mates. A favor from God.

His throat tightened at the memory, and he tried to drink in the air. She was the one woman gifted with the powers to complement his. He hadn't known until too late how much he needed to share his life with someone. And his enemy had murdered her.

She must be the reason the tree summoned him.

He narrowed his eyes, scrutinizing the grounds for yet another assassin. But the only ones there were the Grants.

Uncertain what to expect, he watched, fisting his hand with a vow.

This time he would protect her. This time he would fulfill the promise of a lifetime mate. This time she would be his. Forever.

Emma's brow furrowed as her hand swept along the bark of the tree. *His* tree. "Did I come here as a girl?" she asked. "I seem to know this place."

"I don't think so, child. Your father didn't wander much south of the ravine. Claimed he got bad vibes here. Always afraid, that boy. Not enough faith. Of course, there were all kinds of stories bantered about back then. Some about a man being killed out here, tales about witches and ghosts, you name it. The place became run-down. But with the city rejuvenation and cleanup, well... As you can see, things are different now."

Indeed, things had changed, Venn mused. His mansion lay south of the park, far enough away so as to not attract visitors. A strategic plan he'd sanctioned to assure his privacy. Back in the day, he'd met with wealthy plantation owners and connected politicians on his own terms. Otherwise, he'd avoided them. As time passed and with the never-ending urbanization, he didn't care for the coziness.

When Emma pulled her hand away from the bark, it was like part of him flickered, then snuffed out. He got a mild case of shakes, and his temperature plummeted.

"It's getting late. You must be tired," Mrs. Grant said.

"Nah. I'm a night person, remember? How

about if we stop by Aunt Fay's Coffee Shop on the way home? I've been dreaming about one of her famous cinnamon buns all the way here."

"Okay. You drive." Grams hitched the small dog she held higher under her arm.

They were leaving. With a leap, Venn stood, banging his knee on the side table. He winced and beat back a wave of anxiety. He'd been given a second chance, and he'd be damned if he'd let her out of his sight this time. At least, not for long.

Keenly aware that she wouldn't know him in this life, he needed to initiate a meeting. This minute. However, walking up out of nowhere in a shabby park might scare her.

He wished they could simply pick up where they'd left off.

He envisioned her smiling at him with recognition and running into his opened arms.

But as she got closer to the car and farther from him, the vision scattered.

Aunt Fay's. That was it.

He could use a jolt of caffeine.

As Venn pelted across Aunt Fay's parking lot, loose pebbles crunched beneath his feet. The Tyler streets were fairly deserted, with most people in bed by nine on a workday like today.

He paused to watch Emma through the store window, noting that Mrs. Grant had chosen to wait in the car with her dog. His anticipation mounted.

When he entered the shop, her scent grabbed him—plumeria and cinnamon—an instant turn-on. Even the heady aroma of coffee couldn't rob him of her sweet, luscious fragrance, a perfume he'd profoundly missed. He drew a deep breath as he stepped behind her in line and enjoyed the sound of her voice while she spoke into a cell phone.

Instantly, she seemed to sense him as she stopped mid-sentence and turned.

He smiled and couldn't help but flirt with her. "Something with whipped cream?"

She narrowed her eyes and angled her cell away from her ear with an incredulous nod. "Excuse me?"

"To drink."

"Oh." Her cheeks flushed a pretty pink. "Yes. Umm, and your recommendation is?" She cleared her throat, her green eyes now glinting with pale fire, and then her brows pinched as if she were trying to recall something.

Was it possible she recalled *him*? That would make things so much easier. He was already finding it difficult to behave as though he didn't know her.

"Anything with chocolate," he answered as his lupine senses went into overdrive. Her fragrance intensified, warmed, indicating to him that her body knew what her mind did not.

Her subconscious recognized him.

She gave her head a shake, confusion painted on her face. "Sorry. I…" She paused a beat, steeling her features, and then pointed to her phone.

Her voice drove him to the brink of desperation. He wanted to get her alone. He needed her to remember what they'd shared.

And his beasts concurred with a beat of wings and hammer of paws.

"Miss. What would you like?" the clerk behind the counter asked.

She faced forward again, leaving him to stare at her long, sleek, shimmering hair. He'd kill to slide his fingers through those rich strands.

"For some reason I'm craving something I haven't had before." Her voice was soft and sweet. "A mocha latte. And forget the calories. Add on some extra whipped cream. Also a cinnamon bun, to go."

He swallowed. He had cravings, too, ones he hadn't given in to for a very long time. "Good choice," he said to her back.

Now to convince her of a few other things…

Hell, she'd fallen for him before, she would again.

Remarkably, she seemed eerily the same as the woman he'd known all too briefly. Just modernize the setting and dress—her red-tinted hair, the perfect, to-his-shoulder height, her lovely mouth. He wondered if she'd see the resemblance given the chance.

With the briefest glance at him, Emma stepped to the pick-up line. Venn swiftly placed his order, telling the clerk he'd have the same.

As he came up behind her again, she broke off her phone conversation. "Todd, sorry, I'll call you back. I have to get my order."

Todd? Jealousy surged through his inner wolf, the idea of her even chatting with another male unbearable. His hawk flexed and curled his sharp talons. Fighting to keep control of his body, Venn rolled his shoulders.

While he got it together, the all too efficient waiter handed over Emma's drink and to-go bag. She removed the lid, dropped it in the trash, and sampled the fluffy white cream. A died-and-gone-to-heaven expression lit her face.

Venn suppressed a groan. Then the sway of her hips as she walked toward the door came, nearly driving him wild.

Oh hell. This wasn't going as he'd imagined.

He stepped out of line. "Excuse me! Emma?" he called after her.

She paused and glanced back.

"Sir, wait. Your drink," the man behind the counter said.

Venn could care less about the joe, but he grabbed his order, thanking the guy, and caught up to her.

Her brows pushed together harder. "Do I know you?"

"No. But I know you. You're the sculptor." He smiled at her, trying to put her at ease.

"Yes," she said, pride resonating from the single word.

Aw, that voice. The glue that held him together melted as if put to a blowtorch. A long-ago picture of her naked, full body pressed against him flickered through his mind. The temperature in the room spiked. The latte she held frothed and boiled over.

"My God," she gasped.

Her exclamation hit a tripwire that made him regain focus. He grabbed the cup from her hand, noting in his peripheral vision that the other patrons were experiencing identical problems.

"I've heard of this. A sudden rise in barometric pressure," he lied, knowing full well exactly why the tables closest to him encountered the worst of the damage. The means of discharging excess energy that had built up inside of him just from being near her had explosively discharged.

Surprise lit her face. "How did you…? Man, you moved fast."

He shrugged. Hell, being near her messed with his powers and made them hard to control.

Steam rose from the coffee cup, and he swirled the remaining liquid, then set his drink aside. He snatched a napkin from a table nearby and dried the outside of hers. "Here," he said, handing it back. "This should be fine now. Maybe a bit hotter, so take care."

"Thank you." Her body tilted slightly closer to him.

"You're welcome. Now, in exchange for saving you from having coffee all over your clothes, will you have dinner with me tomorrow night?"

Her eyes widened, and then she glanced down.

"Forgive me if I'm overstepping," he quickly added. "It's just that I don't like to dismiss opportunities when they arise." And he had a major rise happening down south.

She looked down, sunk her teeth into her lower lip, and lifted her shoulders.

Damn. She was going to refuse. He held his breath, waiting for her response and feeling like the world balanced on the tip of her finger.

About the Author

LARISSA EMERALD has always had a powerful creative streak. Whether it's altering sewing patterns, making minor changes to recipes, or frequently rearranging her home furnishings, she relishes those little walks on the wild side to offset her otherwise quite ordinary life. Her eclectic taste in books covers numerous genres, and she writes sexy contemporary romance, paranormal romance, and futuristic romantic thrillers. But no matter the genre or time period, she likes to put strong women in dire situations where they find the men who will adore them beyond reason and give up everything for true love.

Larissa is happy to connect with her readers. Stop by and say hello on her website, Facebook, Twitter, or send her an e-mail.

http://www.larissaemerald.com
http://www.facebook.com/larissaemerald
https://twitter.com/LarissaEmBooks
larissaemerald@gmail.com.

Made in the USA
Columbia, SC
26 May 2018